The Temptress Four

ALSO BY GABY TRIANA

CUBANITA

BACKSTAGE PASS

GABY TRIANA

The Temptress Four

HARPER TEEN
An Imprint of HarperCollins*Publishers*

HarperTeen is an imprint of HarperCollins Publishers.

The Temptress Four
Library of Congress Cataloging-in-Publication Data
Triana, Gaby.
    The Temptress four / Gaby Triana.—1st ed.
        p.   cm.
    Summary: Four best friends embark on a Caribbean cruise the day
after high school graduation, despite a fortune-teller's ominous warning
of strife and storms ahead.
    ISBN 978-0-06-088567-0 (trade bdg.)—ISBN 978-0-06-088568-7
(lib. bdg.)
    [1. Best friends—Fiction. 2. Friendship—Fiction. 3. Coming of
age—Fiction. 4. Fortune telling—Fiction. 5. Caribbean Area—
Fiction.] I. Title.
PZ7.T7334Tem 2008   2007038742
[Fic]—dc22   CIP
                                                       AC

Typography by Andrea Vandergrift
1 2 3 4 5 6 7 8 9 10

First Edition

For the Guids.

"You don't choose your own family. They are God's gift to you, as you are to them."
—Desmond Tutu

THE NIGHT BEFORE
BAY HIGH GRADUATION FAIR—

*T*hings were about to change.

How I knew that, I don't know, but during the closing hour of the fair, I felt different. Very different. Maybe it was the heavy June humidity, or the lights and screams from the midway, or how the four of us clung together, laughing too much, like nothing would ever come between us, but something big was going to happen. It had to—high school was officially over.

We were standing in front of the Ring of Fire, watching the last of the seniors sneak in a final ride, when I saw it, tucked away behind an elephant ear stand. A blue-and-yellow tent with a hand-painted sign: MADAME FORTUNA CAN SEE YOUR FUTURE! 5 TICKETS!

"Let's do this," I told the girls. It was either that or the basketball toss, the only two things we hadn't done yet, and basketball tosses were so rigged.

Killian scoped the landscape for any eye candy she might have missed, but it was getting late. All the cute guys had left for the parties around town. Her gaze fell on the sign I pointed out. "A fortune-teller, Fiona?" She reached out to grab my hair, twisting it into a tight coil.

I counted the tickets I had left. "Come on, I've never been to one."

"All right, it might be fun," she said, letting my hair fall against my back. "I love your hair. I'm going to dye mine reddish brown like yours."

"Don't you dare," I told her for the millionth time in eight years. Switching from natural golden blond to brown was crazy talk. But then, Killian was always crazy talk.

"Auburn. Reddish brown is auburn," Alma corrected, drawing on her cigarette. "I'm game for the fortune-teller thing, Fee, but can I finish this first?"

"If you must." I wished she wouldn't smoke so much, but I knew better than to tell her anything. Both her grandmother and mother were smokers too.

"What about Mo's party?" Yoli whined. She looked especially cute tonight, short shorts with a tight tank that hugged her petite frame.

"We can't. We have to get up early," Alma reminded her.

"We'll leave right after we do this." I watched Mr. Sanders bite into an ear of buttered corn. It was always weird to see teachers outside of school, having fun with other teachers, playing hooky from responsibilities. Reliving glory days or something.

But for me, these really were glory days, and I was painfully aware of that. I kept staring at everyone, trying to record each detail and not let go. I even stared at Missy Fulton, absorbing everything about her: her plus-size jeans, the pimples on her face, her thick wrists, the way she laughed with her friends. What would she look like at our ten-year reunion? Would I ever see her again?

"I can't believe tomorrow's the day," Yoli said, breaking my trance.

Killian stared deeply at the midway as we wandered toward the fortune-teller's tent. "How long have we been waiting for this cruise already?"

In the morning, we were setting sail on the *Temptress*—the newest ship from Caribbean Cruise Line. A celebration for graduating, for staying friends through the years somehow. It was going to be the most amazing, memorable trip, I just knew it.

"Since March." I watched the double Ferris wheel lunge forward with only one couple on it. "Three . . . long . . . months."

From the roller coaster, a shrill cry descended as the train made the steep drop. Killian's hazel eyes reflected the bright white bulbs of the pizza stand. "I hope it'll be fun."

"It better be." I searched the girls' faces. My voice wanted to waver, but I held it steady. I was not going to cry. "It's our last chance to be together."

Yoli looked wounded. "Fiona, that is not true, and you

know it. We *will* see each other. School will keep us busy, not apart."

I wanted to believe her. From the time Yoli and I became best friends in Mrs. Perry's fourth grade class, I figured we'd always be together. We were in the same after-school class, too, where we met Alma and Killian. We started a club called Tough Cats. Stupid, because we were neither tough nor cats. So we changed it to The Foursome, but Derek Pickney kept asking how much to watch, which was considerably annoying, even though we didn't know what he meant at the time.

"Yoli, don't get your hopes up. We're going to be spread out all over the place," Alma said, digging a hole in the muddy grass with the toe of her overworn black boot. Black boots in June—so Alma.

"Speak for yourself." Killian was the only one without college plans. She'd be the only one still home in August. Although her parents' money could get her into any school she wanted at the last moment. *If* she wanted to, that is.

Yoli tucked her loose brown curls behind her ears. "Well, I don't know about you, but I'm coming home every holiday, and long weekends too."

"Yes," Alma said, shifting from one cool pose to another. "But Tallahassee is closer to home. I'll be in Rhode Island, Fiona in New York, Killian who knows. . . ."

"Whatever, *chicas*," I said, wishing Alma would finish the cig already so we could get our fortunes told. "We'll work something out."

"So, what do you think this lady will say?" Yoli asked, bouncing around like a little kid.

"Maybe you'll meet a guy on the cruise and do him on the first night," I said, knowing the chances of such a thing happening were slimmer than Yoli's size-two jeans. I looked over at her and saw her cheeks were pink. "Ha-ha, just messing with you, Yoli."

"It could happen." She smiled, but I could see I'd hit a nerve. Not that any of us were sexperts or anything—well, at least not Yoli, Alma, or I—but it was fun to watch Yoli squirm.

Alma chuckled. "Sure it could, *mama*." Alma herself swore to keep things at third base, saving herself for the perfect guy. Not what you'd expect from such a tough chick, but I admired her for it.

Yoli never minded our teasing much before, but tonight she seemed different. Tonight her eyes dared me. "No, wait. Maybe she'll know if Fiona will cheat on Lorenzo during the cruise."

"Ooh!" Killian bent over like she got punched in the gut.

I clucked my tongue. "It's okay, you'll get yours." I blew Yoli a kiss.

After my fight with Lorenzo the other night about going on the cruise without him, I told Yoli I'd cheat on him, even though I never had in the two years we'd been together. I wasn't serious, I only wanted to see her reaction. Much to my surprise, she seemed to think the idea was worth pursuing on the basis that he'd become "a macho ass" lately. And I couldn't even retort. It was my can of worms I'd opened, and she was free to play with them.

Everyone was staring at Yoli. Then she sighed above the silence. "Why is it whenever you guys say something, it's hilarious, but when I say something, it's not funny?"

"*I* laughed," Killian blurted.

"Because it's not your personality," I said to Yoli.

"Well, I'm tired of everyone thinking that. You know what? I'm going to start fresh on this cruise." She looked so serious, it made me want to laugh aloud.

"What are you going to do, Yoli, start acting crazy?" Killian smiled at Alma.

Yoli raised her eyebrows. "Maybe."

"With your brother there to check on you?" I stifled a huge laugh. "I highly doubt that."

"At least he's going, or else *we* wouldn't be able to go."

Well, that much was true. Santiago and his wife, Mónica, were coming with us tomorrow. Someone twenty-five or older had to accompany us—cruise regulations. So they offered to take a week away from their three-month-old baby girl just so we could go, which was pretty nice of them if you ask me.

Killian smoothed her shorts out and patted her annoyingly flat stomach. "So, what crazy things are you going to do, Yoli? Tell me." She waited for some examples, but Yoli's cuticles were taking up lots of her attention.

"Have toast at breakfast," Alma said. We all laughed because Yoli would never. I always tell her it's about moderation, not low carbs, but she never listens.

"You guys are so hilarious." Yoli stepped up to the tent's flaps and tugged on one of the tether ropes. "We'll see what happens."

Yes, tensions were definitely running high, either because it was our last day of high school, or because we were about to start our last few weeks together. Or maybe because we were waiting to talk to a woman who called herself Madame Fortuna. I wasn't sure.

"Guys," I said to my girls, and their eyes fell on me. "Give me." I held out my hand, palm down. We started this in middle school but hadn't done it since we were juniors. They placed their hands on mine anyway: Yoli's first, then Killian's and Alma's. "Yo, Kill, All, Fee . . ." I said.

Familiar smiles. Killian giggled like she was still twelve, which looked funny since she was the tallest of us. "Forever friends we will be!" they answered together. We laughed like the doofs we totally were.

The girls who had gone into the tent before us emerged arguing, one of them wiping away tears. What had Madame Fortuna told them? Apparently, it wasn't good. Alma tossed her cigarette butt on the dying grass and crushed it. "Time to see Madame *Fart*una."

We giggled and ducked through the tent's flaps one at a time.

Inside, a single lightbulb hung from the middle of the top of the tent. A woman sat at a folding table with her back turned to us, shuffling some battered tarot cards. The frayed edge of her long, beaded skirt brushed the dirt floor below.

"Ree! Ree! Ree!" Killian imitated the eerie sound from that old black-and-white movie *Psycho*, where the lady taking a shower is about to become a dead lady on the bathroom floor.

"Shut up, Kill," Alma scolded.

Just then, Madame Fortuna's head whipped around, and *holy moly*. She could not have looked any fiercer if she were holding a dead animal in her mouth. Charcoal black hair, no shininess whatsoever. Brown eyes surrounded with dark gray shadow. Eyelashes clumped with mascara. Lips, bright pink, lined a quarter inch on the outside. She might've been a hundred and fifty years old. She might've been a zombie.

"May I help you?" she asked in some European accent that sounded fake. She was probably from Trailerville, USA.

"How many tickets for a reading?" I knew the sign outside had said five, but it's just that her stunning beauty threw me off.

Madame Fortuna's wrinkled fingers spread open to show five. Her scowl told us we were wasting her time.

"That's more than the Ring of Fire," Alma scoffed.

The fortune-teller tapped her cards impatiently. "I'll take fifteen for the four of you."

"Ah, a bargain," Killian muttered, collecting all our tickets and handing them to the soothsayer in need of an extreme makeover.

Madame Fortuna shoved the tickets into her apron without counting them. "Sit."

"There're only two chairs," I pointed out.

Madame Fortuna gave me a hard look. *Yikes.* She motioned to some folding chairs in the corner. Yoli helped me open two more. We sat down and scooted close to the table, exchanging wide-eyed glances.

I think we were all expecting some normal-looking lady who somehow knew things, but this . . . this was goth. Madame Fortuna straightened her deck of cards, then began shuffling them again. Killian's grin died, Alma donned her usual bored look, and Yoli stared at the fortune-teller like

Bambi at Godzilla's suppertime.

Then Killian lifted one of her perfectly shaped eyebrows at me. "This better be good."

Hello? The lady is right there, I tried replying with my Look o' Hurt.

Madame Fortuna stopped in midshuffle and laid an eye on Killian. "If you jest," she warned with a throaty voice that had probably seen one too many cigarettes, "the reading will be invalid." Behind her, a fan clipped to the tent frame whirred above the dead air.

This would've been a good time for everyone to stay quiet. But noooo. "We're not jesting," Alma spat with the same attitude that had landed her one detention after another in school. She stared at the woman like she wanted to squash her.

I swear, Madame Fortuna's face was something out of a Stephen King novel. "Young lady," she drawled, "your negativity will one day be your downfall."

Whoa.

Killian lowered her head. Good thing she didn't lose it, or I might have, too. And who would want Madame Fortuna banishing them to the fires of Hell? I covered my mouth with my hand and focused on the cards. *Please get this over with already.*

Like she heard my thoughts, Madame Fortuna placed the cards faceup on the table in what seemed no particular order. Wasn't there some kind of protocol to a tarot reading? I watched her face for signs of foretelling, but she gave away nothing. Just stared at the cards.

She was starting to creep me out. She looked dead. Dead

with eyes open. *Maybe she's fallen asleep.* Killian, Alma, Yoli, and I glanced at one another. No one smiled anymore. No one moved. We just shrugged. Maybe we should've used our tickets for another go on the roller coaster.

Alma leaned forward to peer at the cards. "See anything?"

Yoli nudged Alma's arm to quiet her. Suddenly, Madame F. lifted her hands and placed them on mine and Yoli's, freaking me out for a second. It reminded me of a horror flick where wax dummies came to life. I admit my heart leaped inside my chest, but that was just silly. A part of me wanted to smile just to calm my nerves. Then I noticed how her fingers felt on mine: soft. I thought they'd be dry or cold.

After a minute, Madame Fortuna placed her hands on Alma's—ivory, wrinkly skin over warm brown. Alma stared down at the hands. I expected her eyelashes to flutter in sarcasm, but instead, she looked into the old woman's face real serious. Finally, Madame Fortuna gestured for Killian's hands, and Kill gave them up without hesitation. No more playing around.

The fortune-teller closed her painted eyes.

We waited. And waited.

Normally, something like this would've sent us into fits of laughter, getting us into trouble in classes, but this time, we were too edgy to flinch. We wanted answers, to know what the summer and rest of the year would bring. The future was on all our minds. I didn't need a fortune-teller to know that much.

The old woman finally opened her eyes, letting go of

Killian's hands, and her gaze fell on a card. "The Fool," she said, pointing to it with a long nail. "There will be a voyage."

What? How did she . . .

Killian's eyebrows shot up. Her mouth started to form some words, but the gypsy stopped her with a hand.

"A voyage at sea," the woman continued, still looking at the card.

The hair on my arms stood up. I couldn't believe what I was hearing. Someone must have gone in before us and told her about our cruise. Killian. Killian would do something like this.

Madame Fortuna showed us more cards: a heart with three swords piercing it and a brick tower ablaze under a cloud of heavy smoke. "Eight days of strife . . ." She paused to take a deep breath. The air smelled like cotton candy, butter, and gasoline. "Strife and storms."

"Strife and storms?" Alma interrupted and looked at all our faces for some kind of explanation, but we had none.

"Bonds will be broken," Madame Fortuna went on. Okay, this lady was bogus. How would she even know we had a bond? What if we were random classmates who met up at the fair? I was feeling pretty light-headed right about now. It was hot and stuffy inside the tent. Too many of us in here.

Finally, Madame Fortuna pointed to another card: a dragon dying from a sword wound. On the bottom, I barely made out the upside-down word. But when I did, it made my heart lurch inside my chest: DEATH.

Okay, this stopped being a good idea right about now.

I wanted to get up and run, but we just sat there, watching Madame Fortuna in silence. Her closed eyelids quivered in a way that made me want to pull the covers over my head, but there were no covers. She leaned back in her seat, and as long as I live, I will never forget her empty gaze or what she said when she reopened her eyes. "One of you"—her voice was flat, defeated—"will not come home."

12:38 A.M.
DROPPING OFF YOLI—

"It wasn't me!" Killian cried as we all hopped out of her truck in Yoli's driveway.

"Well, if it wasn't you, then who was it?" I asked. This was too much of a coincidence. It was another Killian prank, I just knew it. Like the time she jumped off the highest bleachers during the Sharks' halftime show and nobody could find her until she showed up at our friend Hamin's post-game party.

"Yeah, you're the only one who would play a joke like that," Yoli argued boldly.

Killian did a little stomp that reminded me of how immature she still acted sometimes. "It wasn't me. Going in to see that lady was *your* idea, Fiona, not mine!"

I folded my arms across my chest. "You might have gone into the tent beforehand and told her anyway, knowing I'd probably want to do a tarot reading."

"What? That is extremely retarded thinking! I was next to you the whole time!" She looked genuinely offended that we were accusing her. I always knew when Killian was lying. Something creeps into her face, like the corners of her mouth fighting to stay firm. There wasn't any of that now. "Of all the bad press you could give me, Fiona." She made a weird sucking noise. "Goddamn."

"Look," I started. "It's not that we don't believe you—"

"It's not?" she blurted, bumping hard against the side of her car.

Okay, so it wasn't Killian. She was way too defensive. So the lady really knew about our cruise? I rubbed my eyes. This had been a seriously long day, even before we got to the fair. And then that woman had to go and say what she said. I let my arms plop against my side. "It's just . . . I don't know."

"Good one, Fee." Killian folded her arms and eyed us all. "Here's what I think. . . . I think she had some psychic ability, fine. She knew we were going on a trip, but the rest she probably made up just to scare us."

"Yep," Alma mumbled, crushing yet another stinkin' cigarette on the ground. I was sure Yoli's mom would screech in the morning upon finding it there in her driveway. "That's her bread and butter, that little scary act of hers."

"Maybe," I said, leaning next to Kill. "But here's the thing. What if she's right about the rest of the prediction too? What if something bad is going to happen to one of us?

I mean, you guys saw the card." God, I didn't even want to mention it again. It was too creepy.

"I know, it was scary. Augh!" Yoli bit at her nails furiously. "You shouldn't mess around with people like that. In fact, we shouldn't have even gone in there."

"Well, then we never would have known what she said. Maybe it's good that we went in. Maybe she was warning us, in which case it'd be stupid to go tomorrow," I argued, even though I knew the chances of abandoning the cruise idea were next to zilch.

"No," Killian said. "The stupid thing would be to cancel a trip we've been planning for three months because of something some freak show said. I don't care what came out of her mouth, I'm still going on that ship tomorrow morning."

"Exactly," Alma added. "I'm not canceling either. I've waited too long, and besides, she probably overheard us talking about it in line for pizza or something. That's how carnies work."

Yoli looked at them with disbelief. "I can't believe this. If we each had half a brain, we wouldn't go."

"Well, I don't have half a brain." Killian laughed, looking at Alma.

"Me neither." Alma put her arm around Killian's waist and leaned into her. "Can we go to sleep now? I'm tired."

We were quiet for a moment—a silence that ended in them all looking at me, like I was the tiebreaker or something, confirming that I had perhaps become the mama hen in this group. Which was just fantastic. What if I said, "Yes, let's go," then something bad happened to one of us? Could

I live with that? But what if I said no, then we missed out on the trip of our lives? On our future memories?

Ack! Decision making sucked.

"Fiona?" Alma said. "What do you say? My feetsies are hurting standing here."

I sighed. When in doubt, use balance, use common sense. Use . . . the Force. "Girls," I said, "let's go to sleep and forget about all this. We'll go on our trip tomorrow as planned, and we'll just keep an eye on each other, and that's it." *There.*

"Fine," Yoli said, all glib. "But if one of us ends up dead, I'm going to blame the rest of you."

Killian chuckled. "Unless the dead one ends up being you."

Yoli's mouth literally dropped open as she stared at Kill. "That is not funny," she said, and walked away toward her front door, jiggling her keys.

"What? It was a joke!" Killian laughed, and Alma added her own smile. "Come back here, dummy!"

"Good night," Yoli said, her back turned to us. "See you all in the morning."

"Everything's going to be fine," I called after her.

Yoli waved and went in without looking at us again. Killian, Alma, and I stood around staring at one another. There was nothing left to say. We were going. Prediction or no prediction. An amazing, fun time we would have. Long nights of dancing and toasting, of sunsets and Caribbean beaches. And no wacky woman was going to ruin that. So why were my friends still staring at me?

"Fee?" Alma said, her eyebrows raised. "Nothing is going to happen."

"Right," I said, letting out a breath. What else was I going to say? I had already paid for this trip, seeking fun, and fun I would have. Still, I couldn't help but think of what Alma had said: "Nothing is going to happen." *Famous last words,* chica.

DAY 1, 10:30 A.M.
DEPARTURE—

*I*f storms were on the way, you'd never know it. The next day, the sky was like blue cellophane. The turquoise waters of the Port of Miami glistened in the Saturday-morning sun. All last night while packing for the trip, I tried to ignore the fortune-teller's words, but they rattled me anyway. My instincts told me not to believe a carnival psychic, but Madame Fortuna's reading was pretty specific. *Could she be right?*

Maybe the trouble had already started. This morning, Lorenzo was supposed to drive me to the port, but we had a minor problem at my house. In my room, he fingered through my suitcase casually, like he was looking for spare change. "Where did you get this dress?" he asked, plucking out a sexy little sundress I had bought a few days earlier. So much for a nicely packed bag.

"My mom bought it for me," I lied.

"Your mom bought you this?" He tossed the offending dress onto the bed like it had burned him.

"Yeah, why?"

He grunted, hands on his hips. "There ain't no way you're wearing that. Why don't you leave it here?"

"Why?" I stared at him.

He didn't say anything. I think he surprised even himself with that stupid remark.

"Don't be ridiculous. It's just a dress, sweetie." I took the dress and started to refold it.

Lorenzo laugh-snorted. "Yeah. One that you're not wearing on that cruise."

I let the dress slide out of my hands and onto the bed. "Excuse me?" There was a charge in the air between us. It felt like it would ignite with even the slightest spark.

"You heard me." He didn't even wait for a challenge, just started to turn and leave my room.

"You . . . I . . . I can't believe you're being like that! It's just a stupid dress, Lorenzo! I'm not going to hook up with any other guys, if that's what you're worried about."

He stopped and eyed me. I never called him Lorenzo. It was always *baby* or *sweetie*. "I don't care. I've never seen that dress before, and you snuck it in your bag. You obviously didn't want me seeing it, so leave it behind and we'll be cool."

At first, I was too stunned to say anything. Then it hit me how much he sounded like all the other guys in his family, and it pissed me off because I always thought he was different than them. "You're kidding me. I can't believe you're making such a big deal about this!"

"Hey, I'm not the one going off on a cruise with my friends without you, packing away hot little dresses for other people to see me in!"

I wanted to point out the obvious, that he would look a little absurd in a dress, but I didn't think it was the right time. Besides, I couldn't believe we were having this argument in the first place. He'd never gotten this mad over anything before. "You need to trust me is what you need to do!" I yelled.

"Don't tell me what I need, Fiona." And he left. Just like that. So my mom ended up taking me this morning. I should've just left the dumb dress in my closet, and everything would've been fine, but I repacked it after he left. He was being completely unreasonable.

As soon as I kissed my mother good-bye outside the port and passed customs, I'd almost forgotten the whole thing. The *Temptress* was the nicest ship I had ever seen—a pearly, floating city, radiating personality next to the dull concrete port. I imagined how the ship might feel if it were a real person: eager to reach open sea and be free, full of possibility.

I don't know why this appealed to me so much. My future was already mapped out. I was accepted to the pastry arts program of the French Culinary Institute in SoHo. I'd finish within a year, then move back to Miami. I'd work as a pastry chef at a five-star restaurant, marry Lorenzo, whose father owned the chain of local drugstores, Peralta Discounts, and have a family. Never would I worry about my next paycheck. Always I'd be close to home. Yes, my mother had my life all figured out.

Not that I didn't want this, but the plan gave me no room to breathe. It was all *go, go, go!* Besides, last night, Madame Fortuna's reading made me realize I might not know anything about my fate. What if it was *me* she was talking about when she said, "One of you will not come home"? What if I was destined to fall overboard on the way to the Virgin Islands?

I couldn't worry about it anymore. A bunch of stupid cards were not going to mess up my fun. At boarding, Killian and Alma clearly were trying not to let things bother them either. Their laughter contrasted with the calm aura of the old folks ahead of us. We probably looked like annoying teens with no respect for quiet queuing.

"'We're not jesting'!" Killian imitated Alma's back talk to Madame Fortuna last night. "Oh Lord, Alma, that was *so* funny."

"Right?" I agreed, looking around, getting a feel for the other passengers. There were some old people, some our age, some families with kids. My eyes were drawn to a skinny guy with a cowboy hat and sneakers and his blond, fringy-shirted girlfriend. They just looked odd to me, like strangers in a foreign land. I wondered if one of them would end up murdering me or my friends at the end of this voyage.

Augh, morbid thought! Get out of my brain!

Alma turned to me. "Fiona, I was seriously about to crack up when *Fart*una said that."

Yoli peered at Alma over my shoulder. "I thought we weren't going to talk about this, you guys. You don't know if she can hear us right now."

Killian made a *tsk* sound like an egg frying in oil. "Yoli, please. If that lady was really psychic, would she be working the Bay High Fair?"

Alma laughed, a low rolling chuckle. "Exactly."

"You didn't seem so blasé about it last night," Yoli said to Killian. "I saw you, you were scared of her."

"No, I wasn't!" Killian made a face.

"Yeah, actually, you were. You should've seen your eyes," Alma said, suppressing a laugh.

Killian adjusted her shoulder bag with a little hop. "Well, you should've seen yours when she grabbed your hand."

"Maybe we should all think more openly," Yoli said, all spiritual-womanlike. "Some people are sensitive. They can pick up feelings. My cousin has weird dreams, and most of them come true."

"How do you know they come true?" I asked. God, Yoli would believe anything.

"They do!"

"Your cousin is a sucker for attention," Killian said, fanning herself with her boarding pass.

And you're not? I could almost see the words floating above Yoli's head as she stared at Killian. It was a little too quiet. Yoli started picking her nails.

Killian drummed her fingers on the metal railing. "Look, it's like Alma said, she probably overheard us talking. Fair workers do that. They get information and prey on the gullible. Then everyone's all surprised. It's total bull."

"Can we please just forget all this already? I need to have fun," Alma said, rocking back on the railing. An old lady with a gold, quilted purse in front of us kept looking at her.

"Yes, please," I said, shaking out my legs, which were starting to feel numb. "So remember we agreed to keep an eye on each other. No wandering off all alone. Nothing can happen to us if we're all together."

"Speaking of which, Yoli, where's your brother?" Alma asked. Ahead of us, other passengers were beginning to board.

Yoli searched the crowd behind us. "Somewhere."

Killian flipped her boarding pass in her hands. She flashed a flirty smile at someone walking by and we all turned around to look. Two cute guys in tight Ts, about twenty. One blew her a kiss and the other wagged his tongue at her. Gross. The bigger the loser, the more Killian found him appealing, something I never understood for such a beautiful girl. "Woof. Bangable. Check it out."

"I'm checking, I'm checking." Yoli's eyes grew huge too. *Since when?* She's always liked standard nice boys, not tongue-flicking dorks. She leaned into me. "Did you see his smile? Was that not the best smile?"

"The best," I muttered. He was pretty cute, but his attitude killed it for me right there.

"Those guys are fools," Alma said, pushing the railing a little harder. The lady in front of us would chastise her any minute now. She didn't understand that Alma hadn't smoked in over an hour and we were about to board a smoke-free vessel.

"You're the fool," Killian shot back. Her gaze was fixed on the cuter of the two. Light brown hair, blue eyes. "The tall one is hot."

"Yes, that one," Yoli chimed in.

"Please." Alma sighed and rocked so hard the railing sprang back, bumping Grandma's gold quilted bag.

"Excuse me, miss!" she barked.

"Excuse me what?" Alma hissed back.

"You're shoving this and it's hitting me!"

"So move if it bothers you!" Alma retorted, and fifty people turned to look at us. I smiled at the crowd, as if it would do any good. I knew that Alma's bark was worse than her bite. Acting tough was her way of holding herself together after her mom had withered away in hospice a few years back.

The old woman turned back around. Poor thing.

"Relax, *Almacita*," Killian said, putting an arm around her. She had a way of calming Alma down, maybe like tickling a pit bull's forehead when it's focused on . . . oh, a helpless bunny, for example.

"Wench." Alma fumed.

One of the faces in the crowd peered at us over a brochure—a guy with brown eyes. He was really, and I mean, *really*, truly good-looking. Killian would never like him, because, well, he actually might be decent.

"Eight days of strife and storms," Yoli muttered, shaking her head, like the prediction was already coming true.

We inched forward on the gangway. I fought back the idea that we were being herded onto a death ship. "Enough," I warned. "No more Madame Fortuna. It was just a trick." But I had to admit it was a damn good trick. I didn't completely rule out that it was Killian's prank either, even though she hadn't pulled one in a while.

No sooner did we cross over from gangway to floating fortress did a photographer immediately squish us together and step back. "Welcome to the *Temptress*, ladies! Can I get a smile?"

The four of us put on our best college girl grins, and the camera flash went *poof!*

Our cabins were on the Florida deck, a level that looked like the Everglades mated with Las Vegas. We still hadn't found Santi and Monica, but we were let on the ship anyway since we already had our boarding passes. We towed our bags down a carpeted hallway heavy in grass designs.

"Aren't their rooms on the same deck as ours?" I asked, out of breath.

"Right next to us," Yoli huffed. "Huge oversight if you ask me. They have copies of all our keys."

"*Ay*, Yoli." I laughed. "Like you're going to be so wild on this cruise that Santi is going to break in on your hedonistic behavior."

"That's not what I mean," she said, leading us down a narrower hallway. "The oversight is having their cabin next to ours. I don't want to hear *them*."

I tried not to think about that, but my brain wouldn't cooperate. "Ew?"

"Exactly."

Behind us, Killian called out, "I can handle that!" She'd always had a huge crush on Santi, even before she hit puberty, so she wasn't kidding.

Yoli sneered over her shoulder. "Why do you always have to be so gross? Sex is not a sport, Killian."

"It's not?" Killian laughed loud, enjoying the sound of her own voice.

Yoli turned to give Killian an annoyed glance.

Alma groaned aloud. "'One of you will not come home'!"

"Shut! Up!" Yoli snapped.

We reached our cabin and Yoli dropped her bags to run the card key through the slot. The green light came on, and she shoved the handle down.

"Hey, ladies." Santi was there with Monica in his arms. "Just checking out everyone's cabins."

"Sorry," Yoli said sheepishly, although I didn't know why. It's not like they were naked or anything.

Monica smiled. "Don't worry. We weren't doing anything." She brushed her shorts with her hands.

"That's the problem," Santi joked, only I got the feeling he wasn't really. Maybe they'd come on this cruise for more than to help us out. They looked like they needed a break themselves. "Come in, girls."

We pushed our way into the tiny room. "Hey, Fee, we got the room with the window." Yoli bumped her brother's shoulder by way of greeting.

"We?" Santi said, looking back at Monica and chuckling.

"Didn't we?" Yoli looked confused.

"Well, we *are* the chaperones of this excursion, and you are on this cruise because of us," he said. "Why? You girls want this room?"

Yoli looked at me. "You wanna let them have it?" The window wasn't that big a deal, although it let in some light from outside.

"I don't plan on being in here all that much, so why don't we let them take it?" I said.

Santi shrugged and looked at his wife. "I guess we're here, then." If a little window would make Monica look happier to be here, then I wanted them to have it.

We moved to the hallway and separated into the other two cabins. Killian and Alma in one, me and Yoli in another. A few weeks ago, I had suggested we flip coins for picking roommates, but Killian and Alma announced they were already paired up, leaving me and Yoli together. Which was fine—I love Yoli and everything—but I was hoping to avoid her heinous snoring and talk of TV shows we'd outgrown three years ago. *Thanks, girls.*

I unpacked while Yoli went on and on about her brother and his wife and their relationship, and how she wanted to be like them when she got married, and how the baby had only brought them closer together. Interesting. They didn't look like soul mates to me, but who really knew how they were with each other? Even Yoli couldn't possibly know everything.

I set aside khaki shorts and a light blue halter top for our big departure and impending mandatory life-vest drill. Yoli got quiet suddenly as she unpacked.

"What's up, *chica*?" I asked.

She inspected a wayward elastic thread on her pair of what looked like Gap Kids underwear. "What do you think she meant by strife and storms?"

"We weren't going to talk about it, remember?" I started changing into the other shorts and shirt.

"How can we not, Fee? I mean, the woman knew we were coming on this cruise."

Sigh. "Maybe it's supposed to rain. Maybe she watched the Weather Channel."

Yoli dropped her folded clothes into a drawer. "Whatever. You think it's funny."

"Yoli, I don't think it's funny, I'm just not going to obsess over it. What can I do to stop fate from happening anyway?"

She didn't answer. Being the big believer in extrasensory voodoo feelings, Yoli should've accepted that she was powerless to stop anything from happening, tarot reading or not.

"I guess you're right." She sighed. Then, as quickly as she'd brought up the subject, she ended it, standing up straight. "Let's go find some guys."

Pardon me? Yoli going out to find some guys was like Columbus going in search of red onions. What happened to her usual topics, like *Gilmore Girls*'s Rory and her transformation of self? Or the top ten reasons why MGM Studios was still her favorite of the Disney theme parks?

Yoli and boys were simply two things that were difficult for me to imagine together. Maybe she was taking this "fresh start on life beginning with the cruise" thing a tad too seriously.

"Guys for you, maybe. Not me," I reminded her.

Nope, Lorenzo Peralta had me. And right at this very moment, he was pissed that I was even here without him. So I wasn't about to make it worse by scoping out the male population. That was Killian's job. And apparently now Yoli's?

Someone knocked on the door. I got up to open it.

"Ready?" Killian stood there, a huge, mama-jamma, orange life vest covering the bikini top she'd changed into, so it looked like she wasn't wearing anything but the vest and her little purple shorts.

"Where's Alma?" I asked.

"Coming. Ready for our first assignment?" Killian asked.

"What assignment?" I didn't like the sound of that. What was she up to?

"You'll see," Killian said, checking me out. "Wow."

"What?" I asked.

"Nothing. Your boobs look big in that top."

"Yep," Yoli agreed from the bathroom.

"Is that good or bad?" I looked at my chest. I guess it was good. Whenever I dressed sexy, people told me I looked like Jennifer Connelly.

Killian wrinkled her nose. "Are you kidding me, Fee? Come on." She linked her arm through mine. "When the cat's away, the mice will play."

That's exactly the kind of comment that made Lorenzo nervous about leaving me with Killian, but she was just stating the obvious. He *wasn't* here to keep an eye on me. Neither was my mom. And even though I felt a little guilty about that, I smiled. It was about time I started having fun.

DAY 1, NOON
AT SEA—

*T*here's this super-old show called *The Love Boat* that I sometimes saw on TV Land. At the start of each episode, a new cruise gets under way, and the passengers run to the decks and wave good-bye. There's confetti, streamers, the whole party scene. Then everyone starts having relationship problems, which, by the end of the show, are always resolved with some help from the crew and starlight at sea. It was produced by Tori Spelling's dad, and I swear, it's pure television genius.

So how come *our* departure was all about life vests and bumping into one another like molecules? And even worse, loudspeakers kept barking instructions at us. Where was

Captain Stubing? And the confetti? I wanted confetti! And frozen drinks with little umbrellas, and a friendly cruise director telling me that festivities would soon begin on the Lido deck, and—

"Fiona, get over it already," Alma said, snarling. "You're driving me insane with that *Love Boat* crap."

Was I going on that much? I didn't even know I was talking! *Okay, Miss Cold Turkey.* Amazing what nicotine deprivation could do to a person. "Well, it's false advertising."

"That's TV for you." Alma snorted.

Killian laughed. "Don't worry, Fee, the fun will soon begin." She tossed her blond hair over her vest and looked out at Government Cut, the inlet that led out to sea, as it slowly inched by. In a few minutes, we'd be sailing on the Atlantic.

I folded my arms around my orange, inflated chest. If only for fifteen minutes, I could imagine what it felt like to be a double-D like Alma, even though she would have gladly sold her breasts this year for higher SAT scores. I was sweating my butt off. Too many people. Fine, I was complaining, but only because I'd been gypped out of my festive send-off.

"We all just made a big mistake getting on this ship, didn't we?" Yoli said to herself, staring out. "We're all going to end up at the bottom of the ocean."

"Nope." Alma shifted her hip around, desperately trying to make the life vest look cool. "Just one of us."

"Stop it!" Yoli cried.

Alma aimed her voice straight at Yoli's head. "You brought it up!"

While Yoli and Alma bickered, I watched Killian stare at the boats, the pelicans, the blankets of seaweed floating on the water. Something was brewing; I knew my *chica*. "Please, Kill," I whispered. "No stunts today."

"What do you think would happen if I jumped over this railing?" she asked softly. "You think anyone would come after me? Or would you all just smile and wave?"

Alma and Yoli quit talking.

"Go ahead," I said. Even with as many crazy things as she'd done in the past, she wasn't about to jump off a cruise ship. "Try it."

Yoli slapped my arm. "Why do you say things like that when you know she might do it?"

Killian's eyes were still focused on the horizon. "You know me well, Yoli."

I imagined Killian leaping onto the railing in the most superhuman of ways, evil grin on her face, diving into the ocean like a demented villainess, then disappearing into the ship's wake, never to be seen again. But in our heart of hearts, we knew she'd return in a sequel, like good villains always do.

Stupid, right? Then why was my heart beating so hard?

It happened so fast, I couldn't do anything.

Killian sprang up onto the middle rung of the railing, and everyone around us gasped. Her arms were out wide, head thrown back, like Jesus minus the cross. Yes, she'd done this kind of thing before, but hello? This was a moving

33

ship, for the love of chocolate!

Yoli reached out to grab Killian's legs. "Stop it! Stop, Killian!" she shrieked.

"Kill, get down, please?" I begged, anchoring her ankles with my hands. Maybe this was it; it was already happening. Killian would be buried at sea.

"I'm king of the world!" Killian shouted, wobbling back and forth, laughing like this was indeed amusing to anyone except herself.

Yoli started crying. A woman with a straw hat next to us yanked at the pockets of Killian's shorts. "Miss, don't do that! It isn't funny!"

Killian saluted a group of guys on a speedboat flanking us. They whistled. She whistled back. "Wooo!"

Yoli's eyes shut tight, tears squeezing out of them. "I can't—I can't look at her!"

Okay, *la loca* was overdoing it. It was time to reel her in. Alma and I reached up and grabbed Killian by the waist, pulling her onto the deck. "Get down, lunatic!" Alma said, then turning to the stunned passengers, "We can't take her anywhere."

"For real, Killian! What if we get kicked off because of you?" I scolded. I tried doling out apologetic looks, but the other passengers weren't buying it. Even if I wasn't the nut job up on the railing, I was a nut job for being her friend.

"What?" Killian assessed the peace she'd disturbed. "I wasn't really going to jump, people."

"Unbelievable!" The straw hat lady's husband glared at us. He put his arm around his wife and moved away.

"Come on! I'm wearing the life vest! See?" Killian called after them. She tugged on the fabric-covered foam. "I would have floated."

"Idiot," some guy mumbled.

Alma immediately turned around to mouth off to whoever it was, but she couldn't tell who'd said it. Neither could I. "Screw you," she said to whomever. I was beginning to regret the smoke-free environment and its effects on Alma.

Yoli chewed her nails, spitting the pieces at Killian. "You are *so* inconsiderate, you know that? I should throw you overboard myself!"

"Please," Killian said, straightening her life vest, folding her hands in front of her like a good girl. She'd relax now that she'd had everyone's attention.

I sighed. I loved her, I really did. But one of these days, she was going to get herself arrested, killed, or worse, invited to be part of a *Girls Gone Wild* taping. "Another classic Killian moment, brought to you by none other than Miss Edwards herself," I mumbled.

Killian grinned, pleased with her commotion. Even though I was used to her stunts, I had to admit that one had scared me a little. Leave it to Killian to take a boring moment and turn it into a good crap in the pants.

It took Yoli two hours to speak to Killian again. We were out in open water, in line (again) for the one o'clock buffet on the Caribbean deck. So far, this cruise was all about lines and drills. I could've had a more exciting time at boot camp. At least there, I'd be able to watch Killian and Alma do push-ups for their unruliness.

"One of these days"—Yoli used tongs to pinch slices of cucumber off a platter like she was furious at them for not being pancakes or cookies—"you're not going to survive your little stupidities."

Killian fluttered her lashes. "Here we go." She grabbed a plate.

Yoli eyed her. "I know what you're going to say: I'm over-reacting. But you know I'm the one who cares about you the most."

I rolled my eyes and speared some white cheese and turkey. Yoli always thought she was Killian's keeper. All because this one time at the Miami–Dade County Fair, when we were in fifth grade, Killian panicked on the Himalaya—the only time I ever saw her scared of anything. She looked like she was going to fly off of it, but there was Yoli sharing the ride with her, yanking her away from the edge. Ever since then, she credits herself with saving Killian from centrifugal destruction.

"Yoli, you're right. If it weren't for you, I wouldn't be here in front of these fine fruits and ice sculptures." Killian kissed her cheek. "I promise not to do anything crazy for the rest of the trip."

Well, that was nice, but could she keep her promise?

Yoli spiked a slice of ham like it deserved to die. "If you do, I won't talk to you."

"Okay, but don't be a baby." Killian turned to me and winked.

Someone cleared his throat. "You know, if you had fallen, you would've been sucked right into the ship's wake.

Nobody could have saved you." A fine, deep voice. Enter Cute Guy #1 from the port—the one eyeing Killian—in line next to us. When did he cut in line? And more importantly, how did he escape Killian's male heat–seeking sensors?

"You're talking to me?" Killian's pineapple slice dangled off her fork.

"Did anyone else here try to jump off the ship today?" Smile. Very cute. But cocky. Not for me. Not that I could have him, even if I wanted to.

Yoli, on the other hand, needed a napkin to keep from drooling all over herself. I nudged her, and her mouth closed into a smile, drastically improving her mood.

At first, Killian was at a loss for words, but that didn't last long. She smiled her vixen grin. "I wasn't going to jump. I was just giving my girls here a bit of a fright."

Alma snorted. "She thinks she's one of Charlie's Angels."

Cute Guy stopped long enough to glance over Killian's long, thin, Cameron Diaz–like frame. His blue eyes shone. "She looks like one." He made it a point to stare at each of us, too, placing his bets all over the table, just in case any of us took his bait. Yoli smiled at him in a very charming but too-sweet kind of way. He smiled back, but returned his attention to Kill.

Killian put more pineapple on her plate and faced us, away from his view. Her eyes popped open. *I like this guy,* they seemed to say.

No, I mouthed, because Yoli liked him, too, and Killian could have any guy she wanted on this cruise. But old habits are a bitch to break.

"What's your name?" Killian asked.

"Loser," Alma coughed.

Oblivious, Cute Guy smiled a sideways grin. "What do I get if I tell you?"

"Some pineapple?" She held up her plate to him.

"I'd rather dance with you later."

"Maybe."

"Tyler. And yours?" He raised his eyebrows.

"Loser," Alma coughed again.

"Killian." She smiled, then turned an evil glance on Alma.

"Killian," he repeated, letting her name dissolve on his tongue. "I like that."

Next to him, a different friend than the one with him at the port chimed in. "Killian, like the beer?"

We all stared at him. Clearly, he was Ugly Friend. Tyler gave him a stern look. "No, the fine wine, dickhead."

I didn't know what was so funny about a guy saying *dickhead* in front of a girl he was trying to impress, but Killian laughed like it was the most hilarious thing she'd ever heard. "Everyone always says that about me," she said in this really annoying dumb voice.

"They call you a dickhead?" I asked, holding down a smile.

"No. . . ." She whipped around and gave me the evil eye. "They think of the beer: Killian's Red?"

"Oh." I smiled. Someone had to mess with her after what she had done to our nervous systems earlier.

Killian reached for a brioche from a platter near the back of the buffet, and Tyler took the opportunity to check out her back end without an ounce of shame. "Nice," he said under his breath.

Alma and I exchanged appalled looks. Would they quit following us? How annoying! Yoli had soured, too, but only because Cute Guy was checking out Killian's butt, not hers.

Pleased that her pose had elicited the proper response, Killian smiled at Tyler and gave him the once-over as well.

"And your name?" Tyler asked me. Great, I'd end up on Yoli's shit list yet.

"Fiona."

"Like the princess in *Shrek*?" He nearly laughed. It was good that he didn't because I would've nearly hurt him.

Yoli held back a snicker.

I plucked a marzipan petit four off the dessert tray and shook my head. "Wow, I've never heard *that* before." I could hear Alma chuckling to herself.

Tyler grinned, even though I wasn't flirting with him. I hated when people said that. My mom named me after Fiona Cleary in *The Thorn Birds*, her favorite book, but no one ever cared to ask. Not even Lorenzo when he first met me.

"You girls going to the captain's thing tomorrow night?" Tyler followed us back to our table. *Go. Away.* It was a beautiful day to be outdoors, and I wanted to enjoy it with my friends, not this doy-doy.

"Yes, we'll be there," Killian purred.

Here we were, not even four hours into our cruise, and one of the hottest guys had already picked the ripest tomato off the vine. The story of our lives. Yes, we were all pretty and had decent-to-nice bodies, but Killian made the boys slobber. All because she was blond. And tall. And, oh yeah, had that annoying habit of pretending to jump off cruise ships, which would make anyone's head turn.

Still, the captain's thing sounded like fun. I wanted to maybe wear the sexy sundress from this morning's incident. I swear, Lorenzo was acting more and more like his dad every day. Would he stay this way or was it a stage he was going through? Maybe he was just trying to be more assertive. I did tell him one time that I wanted him to make more of our decisions, but I was talking about which Frappuccino to order, not whether or not I could pick my own clothes.

"Great. Then I'll see you girls around." Tyler's voice was as smooth as the water's surface, but it still made me sick.

"See you," I answered. Blech.

"Later, Angel." Tyler winked at Killian while his friends ambled off to find seats.

"Charlie." Killian giggled and winked back at Tyler. There was way too much winking going on. I almost gagged on my brioche.

Next to me, Yoli let her plate of low-carb consumables land on the table with a thud. She had a *cara de mierda*— a crap face, or a jealousy face, or a why-does-Killian-always-win face.

Killian and Alma saw it too and traded looks. "Strife and storms," Alma mumbled, shaking her head. "Strife and storms."

Yoli smacked the table. "Stop saying that!"

We spent the rest of the afternoon getting to know the ship—every deck, the gift shops, the spa, disco, casino. . . . The last two were especially important. If we couldn't drink, legal age being twenty-one, we could at least dance or roll some dice. Let's examine the logic in adulthood at eighteen: Lose all your money at blackjack? Acceptable. Go to war? Acceptable. Have a frozen margarita? Definitely not!

After a while, I started seeing the same people from the boarding line this morning—one was an old couple who looked funny because the wife's hair was almost blue and her husband's was dyed black, as if anyone ninety years old would have jet black hair. I saw the cowboy couple again, and the guy tipped his hat at us. The memory of Killian's earlier stunt seemed to be quickly fading. Sometimes, the four of us held hands, and you could just see guys everywhere doing double takes. Not that we should be scoping, considering this trip was for us, not guys. There would be plenty of time for them when we went our separate ways in a few weeks.

That night, we wolfed down filet mignon, Alaskan king crab, and Chilean sea bass—the best I'd ever tasted. Santi and Monica sat at the table next to us, holding hands, deep in conversation. I raised a glass of wine that Santi and Monica had snuck us from their table, and looked at my girls. "To the Tough Cats," I said.

Killian laughed loudly. "Oh my Lord, I haven't heard that in years!"

"Right?" Alma chuckled heartily. She raised her virgin piña colada, which I was beginning to think was about as virgin as a grandmother of ten. She was too happy. "Here, here!"

"To the Tough Cats!" Yoli smiled, lifting her giant glass of virgin strawberry daiquiri. "Such a dumb name!"

"Hey!" Killian put her arm around Yoli. "It was *my* idea."

"But The Foursome," I said, "now *that* was a great name!" We laughed, because it was, of course, *not* a great name, but everything seemed so great in fourth grade.

Alma snorted. "That was even more retarded."

"What were we, ten?" I asked.

"Something like that." Yoli's smile sagged a bit.

"Eight years." Killian sobered and stared at the silver-ware. "It's been *eight years*."

The way she said it made our giggles quiet down. Eight years was one thing if you were my mom's age, but at eighteen? It was almost half our lives.

We sat there, glasses suspended in the air. I didn't want us to start crying. Graduation was bad enough. We had group-hugged and bawled for an hour, our eyes red in every picture my mother took. We couldn't even look at one another without losing it.

"To eight more," I said, tilting my glass.

We clinked glasses. "And eight after that," Yoli added.

"And eight after that." Alma clinked again.

I looked at my friends, recording everything about them. Yoli with her hair up, all bubbly and cute, T-shirt girl. Alma with thick, silver rings adorning every finger wrapped around her glass and the rest of her ensemble dark, like the velvet lining in a jewelry case. And Killian, wearing a skinny top with shiny beads that lit up her eyes and golden hair.

"Let's focus on us," I said, remembering the cattiness over that fool this afternoon. "While we're still together."

"Yes." They nodded, clinking glasses for the last time.

"To us," I said.

"To us." We drank to our friendship. And at that moment, I would have sworn on anything—even my ready and waiting future—that we'd be together forever.

DAY 2, 11:00 A.M.
AT SEA—

On our second day out in the Atlantic, the *Temptress* was showing off her full ocean liner glory. I wasn't prepared for the sheer power a hundred and twenty thousand tons of steel could generate (I read the cabin brochures), but the ship's beauty and design were incredible. How anything so heavy could keep us afloat was a mystery to me. Then again, my brain made sense of crêpes suzettes, not engineering.

The smokestack and jogging area gave off this superenergetic vibe, powerful enough to rattle my insides. Yet inside the ship, you could easily forget where you were, with all the movie theaters, dinner clubs, and spas—such as Sea of Tranquility, the onboard day spa where Killian's dad's credit card was happily accepted.

We ended up there after breakfast, where Yoli again did not have any carbs. I couldn't believe we were on vacation and she still wasn't indulging in normal food. She was, however, treating herself to a full body massage as a graduation present.

I'm not sure why, but I felt weird getting the massage, a) because I wasn't paying for it and always felt bad abusing other people's generosity, even though Killian's parents truly wouldn't mind, and b) I learned at the front desk that all the female masseuses were busy, which meant some guy would be rubbing his hands all over my naked body— something my boyfriend would *not* appreciate.

"I don't know if I should," I said, watching Killian sign the charge slip.

"Fee, don't worry about it. My folks don't care." She finished off her signature with giant loopy swirls.

She didn't get it. I wasn't worried about her parents as much as Lorenzo and what he'd think of this. I decided not to tell her. She wouldn't understand anyway, being the president of the Who Here Thinks Lorenzo Sucks? Club. I didn't know why she hated him so much. They weren't that different. They were both outspoken, both jerks at times. But both were insecure deep down too. Funny that Killian couldn't see that.

If I said anything, she'd only say, "It's just a full naked body massage . . . why should that bother Lorenzo? And anyway, does he have to know?"

From behind the counter, a Barbie doll with shiny, long brown hair and a crisp, white minidress stepped out and took us to a room that had a trickling waterfall and relaxing music. "Have a seat. They'll call you when they're ready." She smiled with perfect white teeth.

"Thank you," we all said together.

We sat down, and Alma leaned into my shoulder. "Lorenzo, right?"

I stared at her. Maybe she should've challenged Madame F. to a clairvoyance duel. "Yeah, he won't like this."

She shrugged. "Look, you tried to get a girl masseuse, but there weren't any. It's not like you deliberately chose a guy." Alma tried convincing an invisible jury. She was definitely ready for Brown.

"Hey, I might want a guy masseuse," I said, feeling the need to defend myself. I mean, I wasn't a goody-goody or anything.

"It's *masseur* for a guy, not *masseuse*. Look, you don't have to feel bad. Everyone knows you're loyal. Lorenzo should appreciate that." She crossed her legs and shook her foot. "God! I need a cigarette!"

Yes, Lorenzo should know I wouldn't do anything to hurt him. So why was he acting all putzy?

As if she had read my thoughts, Alma raised an eyebrow. "If you feel so guilty, skip the massage."

I stared at the waterfall, hypnotized. I would have to find a way of telling Lorenzo about this. Or I could take the omission route and accidentally not tell him. But that was the heart of our second-to-last argument when I insisted he tell me everyone who called his cell, even if it was just

Oraima, his mom's cleaning lady. Or Jenny. Or Romy.

Sluts.

"I'm dumb, but not *that* dumb." So there. I would have my massage and like it.

Alma laughed. "That's my girl."

Killian leaned in. "What are you guys talking about?"

"Nothing," Alma and I said.

"Oh, that's nice. Yes, let's keep secrets." Killian smirked. Then she pointed out Yoli, who was reading a booklet about the spa. She looked funny, sitting there concentrating so hard.

Yoli sensed us and looked up.

"Fascinating read?" Alma asked.

"Guys, do I have to take my clothes off during this?"

Killian, Alma, and I looked at one another and tried not to laugh, but giggles came rolling out. "Yoli!" Killian cried, trying to catch her breath. "You're the best!"

Yoli gave us an annoyed look. "Why's that so funny? I'm serious! Do I have to?"

"Whatever you want." I chuckled. "If you don't feel comfortable, leave them on. But it *is* a massage."

"Is *this* the crazy thing you said you'd do on the cruise?" Alma asked, her eyes watering.

"You guys just keep it up. Go ahead, laugh at my expense." Yoli went on reading the brochure.

I scooted next to her. "Look, they're professionals. No one's going to ask you for your cabin number when they're done."

"That might not be so bad," Killian said.

Yoli cocked her head. "Is that all you ever think about?"

I wanted to point out that she herself had been thinking a lot about guys lately, but decided against it. No need to get into a fight right before we headed into our private oases of relaxation.

As luck would have it, I was first. An older guy stepped into the room. "Fiona DeArmas?" he said in a German accent. He was maybe thirty and what I'd call older-man handsome. My mom would like him. But he was married, according to the thick gold ring on his finger.

"That's me," I said, getting up. This was going to be weird, like my dad's friend giving me a massage. If I ever saw my dad or his friends, that is.

Killian made a sex-kitten face at me. "See you later, Fee." As if I were getting an erotic service instead of a massage. Ew! Not! He was old!

"I am going to hurt you," I whispered to Killian. My abs tensed. I don't know why I was so nervous. *Relax, this is supposed to be enjoyable.*

I followed my masseur down a long hallway, where we crossed paths with another guy—a very sexy young guy with black hair and puppy-dog eyes. I turned around and saw that he was summoning Yoli. *Lucky!*

My massage guy grinned at me. "My name is Bruno. I will be attending to you today."

"Hi."

"Is this your first time?"

"Yes." God, that sounded so virginal.

"Great."

He showed me into a room with a massage table, a wooden armoire, some plants, and lots of fluffy white towels. But the nicest thing was the gigantic window showcasing the blue immensity of the Atlantic Ocean. It took my breath away. Almost immediately I relaxed, and the massage hadn't even started yet.

"Basically . . ." Bruno began. "You're in control. You tell me what you like, what you don't like, what you want, what you don't want. If you don't feel comfortable with a certain touch, you tell me. Got it?"

"Got it." *How am I supposed to know what I like if I've never done this before?*

Bruno pointed to the armoire. "Your clothes go there. Leave on as much or as little as you want, but I can't get to you if you're fully clothed." He chuckled.

I chuckled back, but looked away at the ocean, the plants, anything but at Bruno, my masseur. My male masseur. My older-man, dad's-friend male masseur. *Gulp.*

He stopped to check a basket by the table for something. Was I supposed to change with him standing there? Or would he leave?

"Be back in five minutes," he said. "When you're ready, lie faceup and cover yourself with that sheet." He pointed to the massage table.

"Okeydokey," I said, which is what a hopeless nerd *would* say.

Bruno smiled politely and closed the door.

I waited a minute, just in case he forgot something and came back in. Then I realized I'd better hurry up or he really might walk in while I was changing. So I quickly took off my shirt and shorts. At my bra, I hesitated. *Lorenzo will kill me, Lorenzo will kill me. . . .* But since I'd never heard of a masseur massaging anyone's breasts, I took it off, leaving only my panties. Lorenzo wouldn't understand any of this anyway.

I lay down on the table and brought the sheet up to my chin. I thought I must look terrified, so I pulled the sheet lower, just over my chest. Then I felt like I was exposing too much, so I put the sheet even with my shoulders. There. Not inexperienced, not slutty. I breathed out a heavy sigh and tried to focus on the vibrations of the ship, the CD sounds of ocean waves crashing onto the shore. I wondered what the girls were up to now. Maybe Killian had already gotten her masseur naked. Maybe Yoli had left her clothes on. Maybe Alma was denouncing spas and their contribution to women's negative body issues.

I almost fell asleep. But at last, Bruno came in, clasping his hands together. "All right, shall we get started?" He closed the door.

"Mm-hm," I mumbled, staring straight at the ceiling. I heard Bruno putting some kind of oil into his hands and rubbing them together. *Mmm, almond-scented.*

"I'm going to start with your neck and shoulders, work down to your arms, legs, and feet. Then you'll flip over and we'll do your back. Pull your hair off your shoulders, please," he said.

I did as he asked, and I have to say that as soon as his warm hands started on me, it was hard to think of anything else. It was professional yet intimate at the same time. I tried to set aside any Lorenzo thoughts and just focus on Bruno. *Ooh, Mr. Bruno. You are such a good masseur.*

"How's the pressure? All right?" he asked.

"Fine."

"Good."

He went on. And the more he kneaded my neck and shoulders, the more I found myself falling in love. With the attention, that is. With letting go, and allowing someone else to take over, to just lie there and accept good feelings. With Lorenzo, I always felt the need to do everything right, to perform, in a way. But here, I didn't have to do anything.

I could get used to this.

All day.

All night.

I could get used to this. Did I already say that?

"Everything okay?" Bruno's voice seemed far away.

"Mmff, gnnn," I replied.

His strong hands worked on my arms. I wanted to take them home and replace Lorenzo's hands with Bruno's, or maybe just take Bruno home instead, what the hell. But darn, he was married, and also my mom's age, so I lay there, pretending to be—okay, fine, his wife, if only for forty-five minutes, while he tugged on each and every one of my fingers down to the tips.

Ooh . . .

Happy thoughts. Puppies, presents, parfaits . . .

Yes. This was living.

When Bruno lifted the sheet to expose my thighs and legs, I hardly even noticed. I was already his. He could see me completely nude and I wouldn't care. The only neurotic moment was when I realized I hadn't shaved my legs today.

But they had still seemed pretty smooth this morning, so I didn't think about it anymore. Bruno didn't seem to care either. In fact, who knew? I was probably making his day just by lying there, being eighteen and in pretty good shape.

I was definitely in a sea of tranquility. So relaxed, in fact, that I hardly thought of Lorenzo and how nervous he seemed about my coming on this cruise with the girls. He had said that Killian and Alma on a cruise together would be too much for me and Yoli to handle, but I assured him we'd be fine, and—

Ooh. Bruno continued on my legs and feet. This was the killer, right here. *Ooh . . . I love you, Bruno*. This cruise was already worth the money.

So about Lorenzo . . .

I lay there for a long time, thinking about the last two years I'd spent with him. We'd started out strong, like any other couple, but things were settling down now. Still, except for erratic jealous moments, like yesterday, I felt comfortable with him. Sometimes a little too comfortable. Like we were married already. Like there was nothing left to discover. Alma told me that's because our relationship was starting to run its course. Which is ridiculous if you think about it, because all couples reach that point where you have to do things to keep the romance alive. It doesn't mean it's over, it just means it's time to spice things up.

At least I thought so.

"Hello?"

I just couldn't believe Lorenzo and I might already be at that point.

"You can flip now."

And we weren't even married yet.

"Huh?" I opened my eyes.

Bruno had the sheet held in front of him, blocking his view of my naked boobs. "Time to flip."

"Oh." Wow, I really was on another planet.

I turned onto my stomach. Bruno laid the sheet over my bottom half, leaving my back exposed. I felt completely at ease. Completely absorbed by his hands melting away all the tension in my shoulders and back. So absorbed that I almost forgot about the view just outside the window. I turned my head to the other side and took it in.

Ooh . . . no worries.

None.

The water was dark blue. The sky, light cerulean. The sun bathing the whole thing in a searing brilliance. The immensity of the ocean was mind-boggling. It was unbelievable to me that explorers had traveled over it hundreds of years ago in crude little ships, getting tossed around by nature's fury. Not knowing if, when, or where they would finally land.

I, however, knew exactly where I'd land. At the French Culinary Institute in SoHo, then back home to begin my life. But for some strange reason, I wanted to feel, if only for a second, what those explorers might have felt: the freedom, the promise of possibility, the uncertainty of it all.

So I closed my eyes and let myself feel.

DAY 2, 9:00 P.M.
AT SEA—

*T*ime to party.

I kid you not when I say that we Tough Cats busted out of the lobby's glass elevator that night looking like music video divas in slow motion. Our outfits were hot, our skin aglow with sun and lotion, our hair flowing behind us like halos ablaze. We were on fire.

And people noticed. Everywhere we went, we got looks left and right. You know you look good when other girls stare at you, trying to figure out exactly what you did to upstage them.

The massages had worked. We were new women, refreshed, relaxed, and rejuvenated. I was enjoying one of the best days of my life—well, enjoying as much as anyone could who's been informed that she or one of her friends would perish over the next few days. That fear was still niggling at the back of my mind. But the day wasn't over just yet. There was still the Captain's Welcome.

We had another great dinner that ended with a killer crème brûlée and a seven-layer chocolate cake. I could easily have spent the whole night in the kitchen watching the chefs prepare these things, but I'd be doing that soon enough in New York.

The captain's name was Dimitris Something, and he showed up long enough to wave at us, then go about his merry way of attending to the engine room gauges or his after-dinner sherry, or whatever it is that captains do in their free time.

Afterward, we strolled around the dining room, trying to get a sense of the competition. I knew we'd agreed on the no-guys thing, but Killian was too hot not to show off. Tonight she wore a black midriff-bearing top and tight black pants that flared out at the bottom, with a long gold chain around her hips that dangled as she moved. Any of us could have felt shadowed by her goddessness, but I didn't. I felt proud and protective. If guys wanted to hit on her tonight, they'd have to get through me first.

Yoli was doing her own thing. I didn't know what that puppy-eyed masseur had done to her, but she was up for the grabbing, too. She wasn't as hot as Killian, but in a flirty red minidress she'd bought last week, she could definitely pick up one of Tyler's buddies. Speaking of which, Tyler said he'd be here tonight, but so far nada.

Alma wore a dark, flowery skirt—very anti-Alma, but it

was a special occasion and, together with her black bouncy hair and big curves, she was looking good in it. I had on cute black capri pants with a green wrap-around top to match my eyes, which made me feel all sultry and sophisticated. Go, me!

"Hey," someone said next to me as we left the dining hall. I turned and saw the guy from the port—the peering-over-the-brochure guy. Up close, I could see he was maybe nineteen or twenty. He had dark hair, light brown eyes, and a smile that almost rendered me unconscious. He was much taller than me, too, which was nice. Lorenzo was the same height as me.

"Hi." I smiled back. I fought the urge to make sure he wasn't talking to Killian instead.

"You look great," he said, like he knew me and hadn't seen me in years.

"Thanks." What was the proper response for this? *You too*? Maybe he knew me and was waiting to see if I recognized him. "Do I know you?"

"Don't think so." He grinned and shook his head. "Unfortunately."

I smiled. I couldn't believe I was standing here somewhat flirting with this guy who was ten times cuter than Lorenzo. He should've been over there trying his luck on Killian, not me. "Well, see you around," I said, all cool, like I didn't care to know his name. Because I didn't. Not one little bit.

When he smiled again, I almost turned to melted *beurre*. "Hopefully," he said.

He walked off and the girls closed in on me. "What did he say?" Yoli asked.

"Just stuff. 'Unfortunately' and 'hopefully.'" I smiled.

"Ah, yes." Killian laughed. "An adverb guy."

"Adverb Guy," Alma repeated. "That'll be easy to remember."

"You didn't get his name?" Yoli asked.

In a daze, I followed Killian to the elevator. "Was I supposed to?"

Killian shrugged. "Not if you're not interested."

"Who says I'm not interested?" I tried pinching her waist, but there was nothing to pinch. "I'm just not allowed."

The elevator door opened, and Alma strutted in. "I won't tell Lorenzo."

Yoli scoffed. "You guys have no respect for a betrothed woman."

Betrothed?

"I don't see a ring on her finger," Alma shot back. As much as I hated to admit, it was true. But give it time. . . . Lorenzo would come through! We'd just graduated, for Pete's sake.

Killian pressed the elevator button. The doors closed, and the view of the lobby dropped beneath us.

I thought about Adverb Guy while the girls talked. It was such a non-event, having a beautiful guy stop and talk to me for seven seconds. It probably wouldn't have even registered on Killian's flirt-o-meter, but for me, it was exciting.

"Where are we going?" Yoli asked.

Killian did a little wiggle. "You'll see."

The Bora Bora Dance Club was on the Empress deck, next to the casino. It was almost eleven o'clock now, and the under-eighteen crowd was getting kicked out. The place was filling with adults of all ages, but mostly twenties and thirties. Even though I thought some older guys were hot, I would never dance with anyone more than a couple years older than me.

Killian and Yoli checked out the place like they were looking for somebody in particular. Tyler, maybe? Not to mess up their hopes or anything, but I was glad he hadn't shown up all evening. Perhaps the tea leaves of fortune swirled in my favor and he'd leave us girlies alone.

"I can't even smoke in a freakin' club. Do you know how ridiculous that is?" Alma ordered a Coke from the female bartender. "And no drinks either."

It was funny how this cruise was turning out to be a nightmare for Alma. I laughed aloud, and she gave me a hard stare.

"Sorry." I leaned against the bar and checked out the scene.

The DJ played a mix of nineties and current dance music. Not quite what they were dishing out on South Beach lately, but the beat was good.

Killian pulled me and Yoli to the dance floor, which was lit up like in that movie with John Travolta about the guy who wants to win a dance contest with the ballerina girl. Alma stayed behind, content to watch. The music got better. The floor got more crowded. A few times I had to politely push away some guys trying to dance up on us. Yoli didn't seem to mind. She smiled and pursed her lips, like some ultrafeminine version of herself. I guess wearing a red minidress could do that to you.

It wasn't long before the floor was packed. Every time the crowd pushed us around so that we were dancing in one another's faces, we laughed like fools. We bumped and grabbed one another to keep from falling. I found myself trapped in one of those moments that had been plaguing me since graduation, where I record the tiniest details of everything. The multicolored sheen of Killian's smile. The curve of Yoli's hips in her daring dress. My friends looked so beautiful. Maybe I did to them, too. Which of us would look the best twenty years from now?

I noticed Tyler before anybody else. He walked in with a couple of buddies, including Ugly Friend, and stood there in his jeans and tight T-shirt, thumbs in his pockets. He immediately spotted Killian, her arms in the air, blond hair swinging over her back.

"Kill," I said, but she couldn't hear me over the loud thumping of the music. "Killian!"

She looked at me, but Yoli looked, too. Great. Now she'd probably think I was trying to match up Tyler with Killian and not her. I pursed my lips to point him out. They both turned, and it was interesting to see the reactions. Killian kind of shrugged and went on dancing in her usual come-and-get-me way. And Yoli sort of kicked it up a notch, like the show was on. I felt sorry for her that she felt she needed to try harder.

Tyler hung back with his friends, looking around the club but mostly at us.

Killian sidled up to me and shouted in my ear. "What is Yoli doing?"

"Dancing?" I responded.

We kept dancing until finally Tyler cut his way right through everybody and made a beeline for us. He smiled his sideways grin at Yoli and me, but wrapped his hands around Killian's waist. She turned to face him. Right away, they started dancing like a couple who'd known each other for a long time.

Yoli made a face. It was subtle, but I could tell she was annoyed. Since this was clearly a good time for a break, I gave Yoli a signal and we squeezed past the happy couple, heading back to Alma.

But Yoli didn't notice that Killian had grabbed my arm and pulled me back in. She pressed her back to Tyler and made me stand in front of her, so that she was sandwiched between us. And just like that, I was sucked into one of Killian's three-way dances. Joy, oh joy.

As gracious as I was, playing third banana, anyone could see that the party was between Tyler and Killian. Maybe I could slip away without their noticing. I tried skittering off, but Killian held me close again, like she needed help bagging Tyler. Didn't she realize she already had him wrapped around her finger? But a little girl-on-girl dancing never hurt anyone, so I let her tilt back my head and twist my hair into a thick rope. Her breath felt warm on my neck, and it might've felt nice if she were, let's say, a guy. I turned my mouth up to her, and I swear, you could almost hear the gasps from the guys watching. In her ear, I said, "My job here is done, now make out with him, not me."

She laughed one of those loud, apology-free laughs. I could feel Yoli watching our *Girls Gone Stupid* thing from the shadows, pissed off as hell, so I said good-bye and bounced.

Whew! I asked the bartender for some water.

"Someone was having fun," Yoli growled.

I eyed Killian and Tyler again. "I was trying to get out of that." I thanked the bartender then chugged down the water.

"She's such an attention whore, it's not even funny."

"Yoli!" Alma turned a stare on her. "*What* is your problem?"

I was used to hearing Yoli's complaints, but Alma wasn't. Yes, we were all friends, but Yoli usually confided in me and Alma in Killian. Not always but most of the time. And whatever Alma heard usually went straight to Killian's ears. Now I realized that's probably what Yoli wanted.

"What? You know it's true. Why doesn't anybody ever tell her?"

I have. I've told her lots of times that she doesn't need to do much for attention, that she could just be a stick in the mud and still get whoever she wanted. But after a while, I just gave up. She was having fun and didn't want to hear it.

"That's just how she is, Yoli. You're not going to change her." Alma stood up straight and arched her back, stretching.

"Maybe one day she'll realize it. When she's tired of playing," I told Yoli above the music.

"Exactly." Alma yawned.

As much as I loved clubs, especially ones where everyone seemed to be having such a good time, I felt crowded. I wanted to get out of there and stroll. Feel the tropical breezes or something. With my hand, I covered the yawn I'd caught from Alma.

"Leaving?" Alma asked, her brown eyes hopeful.

"Yeah. I'm going to walk around, maybe head back to the cabin." If I ran into Santi and Monica, I'd talk to them for a little while.

"I'll come with you," she said, gathering her bag.

"Me too." Yoli adjusted the strap of her dress with attitude. "This could take all night."

No kidding. In fact, we probably wouldn't see Killian again until morning. I was only sorry that now we were left to deal with Bitter Yoli.

We wove single-file through the crowd, past men who stood alone with their drinks. I felt sorry for them watching from the sidelines while guys like Tyler took home the trophies. I bet they were really nice. Maybe Yoli should go for one of them.

Then I wondered if maybe this new side of hers wasn't so much about guys or about Tyler. Maybe it was more than that. Maybe it was a rivalry thing. With Killian as the main enemy. Not exactly the stuff of friendship vacations, now was it?

DAY 3, 8:15 A.M.
SAN JUAN AND FAJARDO,
PUERTO RICO—

*I*t wasn't until the next morning that I realized we had broken our rule of sticking together, but since we were so used to leaving Killian behind at parties, it hadn't registered. Yoli and I entered the dining room to find Alma already having her coffee and a bagel. "Why didn't you wait for us?" Yoli asked.

Alma took her time looking up. "Good morning to you, too, Sunshine. I knocked. Nobody answered."

"We were still sleeping," I explained, glancing around the two-deck-tall dining room. Through the gigantic windows, I saw that we had already docked in San Juan, our first port of call.

"Where is she?" Yoli scanned around.

"Who?"

"You know who I'm talking about; don't play stupid." You could see that Yoli immediately regretted saying that to a woman already upset about not having her morning cigarette.

Alma ripped off a chunk of bagel and cream cheese with her teeth. "She's coming."

"She didn't come in last night, did she?"

"Why would you say that?"

"Well, because when we last saw her, she was humping Tyler while a room full of people watched."

"It's called dancing, Yoli."

"It's called deduction, Alma: We all know where that leads if you're Killian. So did she?"

Silence.

Alma lifted an eyebrow and calmly went on eating. It wasn't like Yoli to get in her face like that. I didn't want to be around when the blood was spilled.

The clinking of coffee spoons and saucers chimed throughout the dining hall.

"I'll take that as a yes," Yoli said, and stomped off to the breakfast bar.

I sat down for a minute. Alma would tell me the truth. "So where is she?"

"When I left, in the bathroom."

"Then she *did* come back last night?"

"Yes."

I blew out a sigh of relief.

"She came in around three."

"Three?" My mouth hung open. I leaned in. "She stayed with him? She—"

"They stayed out on the deck drinking with two of Tyler's friends, but nothing happened. I heard her stumble in, and that was that. I just didn't feel like filling Psycho over there in on the details."

I looked at Psycho, I mean Yoli, piling scrambled eggs, bacon, and sausage on her plate. "Yeah." I stood up. "I don't know what her problem is. Let me go see."

Alma talked with her mouth full. "She's wack, that's what her problem is."

At the buffet, there was so much food to choose from. I was so busy taking it all in that I didn't even notice when Yoli came up to me. "You know what?" She huffed, not really wanting an answer. "I don't care anymore. If she wants to be a slut, let her. I'm over it."

"Yoli, what is wrong with you? You're all pissy lately. Is it because of that guy?"

She made a weird sound, like a laugh-hiccup. "What do I care? He's not even that cute."

Okay, yeah. It was so obviously about him. "You said he was."

She did the laugh-hiccup again. "Whatever. I just want to know one thing: Why can't she give someone else a chance?" She didn't even wait for me to answer, not that I had any spectacular response for that. She just walked off, leaving the thought hanging there.

I scooped some fresh berries and juicy pineapple off the fruit platter. When I got back to the table, I saw what the cat had dragged in. Killian sat, head in hands, sunglasses over her eyes.

"What happened to *you*?" I joked.

She stared at me so long, I thought maybe she didn't recognize me. "Nothing, and before you all start asking, I didn't do anything with Tyler."

The way she said his name so casually made me think that she had at least gotten to know him pretty well. "You don't have to explain anything," I said to be diplomatic, but of course, she would explain, or else why would we all still be hanging around, waiting for her talk?

Yoli started eating. Nobody spoke. "Uhh . . ." I said. "Beautiful day, isn't it?"

Killian played with a spoon. "He kissed me. That was it."

I sipped my orange juice. Yoli tucked her curls behind her ears. I could almost hear her think, *Of course he did. Why wouldn't he?*

"And just so you know . . ." She turned to Yoli, but Yoli stared out the window. "It was hard to leave it there."

Killian sighed and swept off her sunglasses. Her eyes looked a little tired. "From now on, I stay with you guys. I won't go with him anymore."

Good call. I wanted to jump up and hug Killian. She could've easily decided to say "Screw it" and do whatever she wanted, but she could also listen to her conscience when she wanted.

We ate for a while, talked about Puerto Rico and how the last time I was there, it was with Yoli and her mom when we were twelve. We had visited Yoli's grandmother before she moved to Texas. Since we had seen most of San Juan on that trip, we decided that we'd do an excursion today, something outside the city.

Suddenly, it was a little too quiet. The girls had stopped talking, and the whiff of aftershave gave it away. I looked over and saw Adverb Guy squatting by me. "Good morning."

"Good morning," I said, looking back at my fruit. It felt weird to have a guy staring at me so close. Especially one so damn cute.

"You girls having a nice time?" I liked that he didn't grunt when he spoke like so many guys. "Huh," "hey," "what," "right . . ."

"Pretty good," I said. "And you?"

"Pretty good." He smiled.

Augh! Lorenzo, who?

"Well . . ." He tapped the tablecloth and stood. "My name's Raul. Just thought I'd introduce myself."

I felt like an idiot for having run into him twice now and still not asking his name. "Fiona," I said. "And this is Alma, Yoli, and Killian."

"Hi."

"Hi."

I thought for sure his eyes would linger at Killian, but they didn't. For a fraction of a second, they hovered on Yoli, but mostly they stayed on me. "Nice meeting you. So you going into town?"

"We're going kayaking," Killian said. "Want to meet us there?"

I kicked Killian under the table.

She pretended to bend and scratch her foot, whispering next to my ear. "What? He's cute."

"Thanks, but I'm already sightseeing with my people over there," Raul said, glancing back at another table.

"Then we'll see you back here tonight?" Killian smiled.

"Definitely." He glanced around, hands in his pockets, just being genuinely nice. I appreciated that he wasn't staring any of us down or being overflirty. "Well, see you girls later."

"Bye," we said.

"Nice to meet you," I added, even though we went through this already.

He turned around one last time. "Same here." Big grin.

I grinned back.

He wandered back to his group of five people: four guys and one girl. When he was a safe distance away, we broke into quiet laughs. That's all it took for things to be back to normal. The way I liked it: no arguing.

Killian smoothed out my hair and played with the ends. "Someone likes you."

"Yeah, well. Maybe if I was someone else. Maybe if my life was different."

I looked at Alma. Most of the time, she was quiet, but sometimes I could tell just by looking at her if something was a good idea or not. Something like this whole Raul thing. Wise, brooding Alma.

She held her coffee up to her mouth and slowly sipped. Behind it, she grinned at me and winked.

❊ ❊ ❊

We stood near a bus waiting for everyone who had signed up for the excursion to arrive. It was a pleasant surprise to see Santi and Monica with us. We had hardly seen them yesterday, but today they were coming along on the kayak trip. Today they didn't hold hands, and I wondered about that. How sometimes they seemed thick as thieves and other times a little distant, like they'd just had an argument, one that we'd never, ever have the pleasure of listening in on.

Our tour guide was a guy named José. He talked to us about the bay we were going to and how at night, there were microorganisms there that were bioluminescent. Too bad we wouldn't be here tonight. That would've been pretty to see.

We took an hour bus ride, past a famous lighthouse in Fajardo, to a natural reserve called Las Cabezas de San Juan, which meant "The Heads of St. John" in Spanish. We were going to be kayaking in a mangrove channel similar to the ones I'd visited a dozen times at home in Florida.

Good thing we'd worn our bathing suits. It was hotter than hell, and the sun was beating down on us with no remorse. I hadn't had a chance to build up a base tan before the trip, so I slathered on some sunscreen; otherwise I'd be extracrispy later on.

I kept looking over at Santi and Monica. They reminded me of Lorenzo and me together. They had met in high school too and seemed to enjoy being together, but there seemed to be some distance between them. Like they had come on this excursion to get some fresh air. Every now and then, Santi would put his hand on Monica's back to steady her over some rocky ground, and Monica wouldn't even acknowledge him. But at least he was helping her so she wouldn't fall. I'm not sure Lorenzo would do that with me. He wasn't quite as chivalrous. But otherwise, Lorenzo and I didn't seem so different from them. Would that be us in ten years if we got married?

"You want to ride with me?" Yoli asked, startling me. I didn't realize we were already picking our kayak partners. José said something about two people and the weight limit being four hundred pounds. I laughed to myself, thinking that Yoli and I together weren't even two fifty.

"No, I want to be with Yoli." Killian slid between us. "We need alone time." She smiled and put her arm around Yoli's shoulders. Yoli's eyes grew big. She looked at Alma and me like *Help!* But it was nice to see Killian trying to reconnect with her.

I remembered Madame Fortuna's words again. "Bonds will be broken . . ." Obviously, she didn't know what she was talking about. Now that the smoke had cleared, I could see that. Yes, we had separated for a little while last night after the club, but things were fine now. Still, I wondered if Killian remembered her words too and was trying to reverse the prediction.

"That makes you and me, *mama*," Alma said, handing me a life vest. I liked the rare moments when it was just her and me. It was like having a protective older sister around, except she was four months younger than me. For some reason, Alma always reminded me of a less inhibited, stronger version of myself. Like me, but five years from now, maybe.

Where there was water, there were life vests. We put them on and carefully stepped into our rocky kayaks. When everyone was ready, we took off, following José, paddling away in our little yellow banana boats. Killian and Yoli followed us close behind. There was no more fighting, no more cattiness. Just trees, birds, and water. The stillness of the channel filled me with a sense of peace. I don't know how else to describe it. I thought a kayak ride might be boring, since not too many people had signed up for it, but it wasn't. It was awesome.

Too bad Lorenzo was missing this. I was sort of glad, though. He wouldn't appreciate kayaking anyway. It was too removed from his DVDs and computer games. I wondered if Raul would like kayaking. I wondered what he saw in me. Why he kept coming to talk to me. He seemed bored with his friends. Was he as nice as he seemed? Or was he really a jerk? Maybe Yoli should go for him to get her mind off Tyler.

As we glided through the water, I heard the calls of different birds and saw them move among the trees. I also saw some monkeys, the curves of their tails hanging just beneath the branches. The water was clear enough that we could see lots of fish underneath the surface. Puerto Rico felt like Florida but more pristine, more exotic. I wanted to capture it somehow.

I remembered my camera and took it out. "Fee!" I heard Killian call and looked over. The freak was standing in the kayak. "Fee, take a picture!" She posed with a leg stretched out behind her. Was she stupid? Yes, of course she was, but why couldn't I ever get completely used to her?

"Killian, sit down please!" Yoli's voice was full of panic.

"*Señorita, sientese!* Sit!" In a split second, José had turned from informative tour guide to authoritative kayak police.

Killian reached out for balance and placed her feet on the boat's edges. It rocked back and forth violently. "Fee, hurry up and take it!"

"*Oye,*" Alma yelled. "He said there were alligators, you dork. Get down!"

I was frozen. Behind me, I could hear Santi, Monica, and others calling out to Killian. She listened to nobody. I forced myself to frame the shot. Maybe if I took a photo quickly, she'd stop. When was Killian going to stop doing these things and grow up?

"Cut it out!" Yoli was pissed. She grabbed the edges of the kayak, trying to steady it. "Why did I even get in this thing with you?"

Killian rocked the boat harder. Alma was giggling, but I could tell it was nervous laughter. José kept barking at Killian to have a seat, but she was all, "Check it out. . . . Woooo. . . . Yoli!"

"Enough, Killian!" I had to intervene. "You're scaring her!"

But then Yoli shot me a look.

What? I looked back at her.

"She's not scaring me; she's just ruining things," Yoli said, all defensive.

"Well, excuse me!" I said angrily.

Kill clapped once and did a little dance. "I'm livening things up, not ruining them!" She pushed her foot down hard, and I instinctively brought the camera up, snapping the shot.

"Killian!" Yoli cried, but forget it. Too late.

The yellow boat flipped over as expected, and Yoli, Killian, and the contents of their kayak went flying into the river, making a big ol' splash. I snapped one picture after another. There was a lot of commotion. Even the monkeys were yelling at us. *Stupid humans! Get out of our preserve!*

Alma was laughing. I wanted to laugh too, but taking action shots required hand-eye coordination. Plus I wanted to make sure everyone was okay before laughing. Yoli's smushed curls came out of the water, plastered to her head, just as she sucked in a huge breath of air. She smacked the boat and let out a frustrated scream. I took another picture, not realizing that the strap on her bikini top had slid off her shoulder, showing her possessions from under her life vest.

"Yoli, pull up your strap," I said.

She looked down and immediately hugged the boat to cover herself. So Yoli was okay, but where was Killian? She hadn't come up yet. What was she doing, swimming with alligators?

Oh, crap. Alligators!

"Killian?" I cried out. I looked for her everywhere but all I saw was her life vest floating on the water.

"Kill!" Alma yelled. "Shit." She put down her oar and carefully tried standing.

"No, Alma, or we're going to flip too," I said. The boat rocked back and forth. She squatted slowly.

"Esta chiquita, dios mío!" José muttered, starting to take off his shirt. Santi was already diving in the water like an otter. José dove in with him.

A head came up nearby, but it was only Santi's. He wiped the water off his face and scanned the surface. The feeling I usually got whenever Killian pulled a stunt, the feeling that she would come out okay in the end, started fading. She was taking this too far. "One of you will not come home."

Damn it.

"Killian!" I yelled harder, as if she would even hear me underwater. But it was all I could do. Everyone was yelling. This wasn't funny anymore.

All of a sudden, we heard a thrashing noise coming from the opposite side of the river, twenty feet away. We looked over and saw arms flapping, splashing, reaching for shore. Santi and José started swimming toward the commotion like maniacs. Then, a sopping wet girl-woman hoisted herself out of the water and threw herself on a tangled mass of mangrove roots.

Killian cleared the water off her face and snorted some major laughs. "Sorry, Yoli!" she yelled across the water between gulps of air.

I lifted the camera to my face and took another picture.

And another. I wanted to put one in a nice frame when I got them printed. So when I'd find myself far from home and all alone in New York City in the fall, I could look back on this afternoon and remember the way Killian looked. Right before we killed her.

DAY 3, 9:25 P.M.
SAN JUAN, PUERTO RICO—

When we got back to San Juan, there was just enough time to eat and make it back to the ship for a midnight departure. We decided not to kill Killian, on the basis that murder was illegal, plus we were too cute for Death Row. But José, the tour guide, looked as severe as an angry water buffalo, which is something I'd never seen, but it couldn't be good. Of course, Killian solved the problem with a wad of soggy cash for his troubles, and José rode into the sunset a free man.

Santi and Monica needed time to recover, I guess, and headed back to the ship. I hoped Santi wouldn't put Killian on an impromptu flight back home. I was sure with a tighter leash, we could pretty much control her for the rest of the cruise. Still mad, Yoli had wanted to leave with her equally pissed brother, but I convinced her to stay with us and try to have a good time.

She did, but only because I promised to delete her boob picture.

Because our lunches had been in Yoli's bag, which got soaked, we didn't get to eat, and José hadn't been all that sympathetic. So we were starved and on our own. Luckily, there were many places to choose from. We walked along the cobblestone streets of Old San Juan, peeking through restaurant windows, seeking one that had a younger crowd. We heard some guys making a ruckus and saw a group across the road, walking down the opposite sidewalk: Tyler and Ugly Friend with two of their other buds. There were a couple of girls with them I hadn't seen on the cruise so far. One of them had giant, fake breasts and long brown hair. "Hey, there's Tyler," Killian said.

"Whatever happened to natural beauty?" Alma mumbled.

Killian whistled. Tyler was laughing when he noticed her. "What's up?" he said a little too loud, even though the streets were full of people and music was coming from one of the restaurants or bars.

"Nothing. Where you headed?" she called.

"Back to the ship. Wanna come?" He gave her what looked like a secretive grin, like Killian should know what was going through his mind.

"Nah, maybe later."

"You know our deck and number, right?"

"Um . . . not really," Killian said in a voice I recognized as straight-out lying.

Tyler laughed. One of the girls linked her arm through his. What was so funny? "Okay, maybe I'll see you later. Bring your friends." His buddies chuckled at that too.

What was that about? Did she really know his room number? I thought she'd only hung out on the deck with him and his dumb friends.

"Oh, yeah," Alma said. "Let's all go have one giant more-some."

Killian turned back and smiled. "Hey, it could be fun."

"Don't you think you've had enough fun for one day?" Yoli spat, her eyes following Tyler. He was still stealing glances at us and noticed Yoli checking him out. He smiled at her.

I think she smiled back. I wasn't sure since my eyes were going back and forth between them, and the street was dimly lit, though not as dimly lit as Tyler's new chick seemed to be.

Killian put her arm around Alma and me. "You think one of these places might cut us underage lushes a break?"

Yoli huffed. "I know I could use a margarita right about now."

We weren't big drinkers—maybe a beer here and there at Killian's friends' parties—but a drink sounded good. It had been a pretty stressful day.

We looked for a place off the main street, down a little alley where the cruise people wouldn't think to go. We found a spot that was dark inside with lots of locals and good salsa music. They served us frozen drinks without asking for any ID. Not that they were strong or anything, but they were drinks nonetheless. I think the woman bartender felt sorry for us, or maybe she just wanted to make a few bucks on a tip.

The funny thing about alcohol, though, is how differently people respond. You have the funny drunk, which in this case was Killian with her retarded elephant jokes. "What do you call an elephant when it comes out of the water?"

We stared at her, smiles plastered on our faces. Yoli was already laughing without even hearing the punch line.

"Wet!"

It was so stupid. We laughed so hard, turned red, gasping for air. Even Yoli's mood had lightened. Alma almost fell off her stool, and she held on to me for dear life. The sweet drunk. That was her, funnily enough. "You know I love you, right?" she'd say to me every five minutes.

"Yes, Alma. I love you too." I had to laugh. I was glad she was feeling better, now that she could indulge in two vices at once.

Then there was the honest drunk. Guess who?

"You know, Lorenzo can be such a freakin' jerk at times, you know what I mean?"

The girls stared at me. Killian pressed her lips together hard to keep from laughing. Alma was almost in tears. Yoli couldn't believe what she was hearing. "No, Fiona, why don't you tell us?" she said.

That made Killian burst out in fits.

"Fine. Maybe I will," I said, leaning comfortably against

the slick table. "He's smart, he's cute, his dad's rich, and all that. Right?"

"Riiight. . . ." the girls all said.

"But the thing is . . ." I saw their faces crunched together, their arms around one another, waiting to hear what the thing was. I was probably about to say too much, but so what? I'd had three margaritas, damn it, and they probably wouldn't remember a word I said tomorrow anyway.

"The thing is?" Alma's eyebrows were raised, waiting.

"The thing is . . ." I started again, but I really didn't know what the thing was, I just knew something was the thing.

Killian couldn't contain her glee. "She can't put her finger on the thing."

Hoots. Snorts. They were really having a good time with this one.

"Yeah, it's Raul's thing she's thinking about, but she can't do a thing with it!" Alma grabbed a napkin and blotted her teary eyes. She laughed so hard, snot almost came out of her nose.

Even Yoli was in for the kill. "Is that the thing, Fee? You want to try someone else's *thing*?" They howled, and I sat there, smiling facetiously at my supposed friends.

The more I grinned at them, the more they laughed. The thing was I wasn't missing Lorenzo on this trip at all. At first, I hadn't even noticed it. But now I was definitely aware. I looked deep into my margarita. "I don't know. Maybe."

So was that the thing? Did I have a crush on Raul? I

thought he was sweet, but it wasn't like I was fantasizing about him or anything. I just liked the attention I'd gotten from him, that's all. Still, it would be nice to be unattached for one night, to have the choice of getting together with him. You know, like if I wanted to.

When the *Temptress* finally departed, we went on one last walk-through. If nothing interesting was going on, we said we'd call it a night and head back to our cabins. It was already one A.M., and it had been a very long day. But the other thing about drinking is that you want to make the numbness last. There would always be time for sleep when we got back to Miami. So we wandered the ship like ghosts, checking out places and people.

The Bora Bora was still going, but only a few people were inside. The casino was full, though we didn't find anyone worth hanging with.

"We should go find Tyler," Killian said.

"We should," Yoli concurred.

Killian turned to her and smiled sadly. "You like him, don't you?"

"He's cute." Yoli sighed. "But he obviously doesn't like me."

Killian shrugged. "Well, that's probably a good thing."

Yoli's face just sort of froze. We all froze. I had no idea what she meant by that. Yoli folded her arms. "Don't hold back because of me. If you want to do the guy, do the guy." She stormed out of the casino.

Alma and I looked at each other, then back at Killian.

The other thing about drinking is how people don't

hold back like they would if they were sober. We followed Killian into the breezeway, where she caught up with Yoli. "If you think he's so hot, why haven't you talked to him or tried flirting with him? If you don't show him you're interested, how's he supposed to know?" Killian asked.

Yoli stopped and faced Killian cold. "Because look at you!" She gestured at Killian's bikini-shorts-clad hard body. "How am I supposed to get a guy's attention with you standing next to me?"

Killian made a face. "What does that mean? You're beautiful, Yoli."

"Oh, please!" Yoli marched on. "Don't give me that crap. The point is, I'll never be able to compete. You will always be the prettier, taller, more beautiful one. I'll never win against you."

I couldn't believe Yoli was letting this get to her. Killian had always been this way, but *now* was when it bothered Yoli? Then again, they'd never liked the same guy before.

Alma shook her head. "I can't believe you two are fighting over a stupid guy. Let me know when you're finished with this idiot behavior." She plopped into a lounge chair and crossed her feet.

"So what do you want me to do, Yoli?" Killian called. People strolling the breezeway listened in. "You want me to fall off the earth, just so you can get men to look at you?"

Yoli walked farther away from us. Any more yelling and whales would hear them. "Do whatever you want, Killian. I'm going to sleep."

I hung back with Alma while Killian let her arms slap

her sides, frustrated. "It's an attitude, Yoli!" she yelled down the hall. "It's not about looks!"

"That's true," some woman said from her lounge chair.

She was right. How many girls had I seen get anything they wanted with the flick of a pinky without even half the physical advantage Killian had? Still, not everyone was built for commanding attention like that. Especially Yoli. Not that she hadn't tried. She had worn that little red dress last night. She had tried making eye contact with Tyler tonight. And he had looked at her, but only for a fleeting moment.

When Yoli was gone, Killian looked at us. "What is her problem?"

Wasn't it obvious? "She likes him," I explained.

"She's a baby." Alma stretched her arms above her. "But I understand her point."

Killian's face looked confused for a second, like Alma was supposed to be on her side, not Yoli's. "So what, is she going to cry every time a guy doesn't like her back?"

"I think it's more about him wanting *you* than it is about anything," I said.

"And how is that my fault?" Killian threw up her arms. "This is so stupid."

It really was stupid. But at the same time, I understood too. In eighth grade, I liked Brett Volowsky. I was pretty sure he liked me back, until Killian came along, tossed her hair, flashed her smile, and even with braces, it was all over. But with Yoli, it had never been an issue. Yoli's types were never Killian's types. Apparently, the types had now merged. Great timing.

"Why'd you have to say what you said back there?" Alma asked.

"What?"

"That thing about it's good that he didn't notice you."

"Because."

"Because what?" I demanded.

She laughed a short laugh, then looked away, out at the blackness of the ocean. The lights of San Juan were now far behind us. "Because the guy's a jerk."

No shit.

"I hung out with him. I know," she said.

"Okay, so if he's a jerk, why don't we tell Yoli? And that'll be it," I said.

"Go ahead and tell her, but it's not about Tyler. It's about me. She's just mad at me. It doesn't matter which guy comes along." Killian undid her ponytail, then reworked it into a knot. "She's always mad at me now. I don't know what she wants me to do."

Alma yawned. "She's just trying to be more assertive. Let her be."

It was true. Yoli was changing. I guess we all were in a way. "Yeah," I chimed in, "and it doesn't help when you're always acting so freakin' crazy around her. You need to relax, *chica.*"

Killian smiled. "I know." But I could tell she didn't want to. Crazy is all she'd ever be. That was Killian; take it or leave it.

But if Yoli was changing, who would our innocent one be? Who would we tease? If we changed, would we even stay friends? That plus thinking about Killian and why she'd want to hang out with a bunch of guys she called jerks was way beyond me. "Then why do you like him, Kill?" I had to ask. "If he's such a jerk?"

"Huh?" She looked at me for a second, registered what I was asking, then looked out at the black ocean. The wind beat wisps of her hair against her face. "Oh, I don't know. But Yoli shouldn't be with a guy like that. She deserves better."

So . . . didn't she think *she* deserved better?

Alma and I traded glances. I could tell she was thinking the same thing, but was letting me handle this all by myself. I wanted to tell Killian that she deserved better, too. Someone who'd appreciate her. Someone who would love an adventurous girl with a kind heart. A little crazy at times, but hey, nobody's perfect. But somehow I didn't think Killian herself even knew what she was worth or else she wouldn't try so hard to convince people.

Killian snapped out of her trance and leaned back on a column. She smiled, but it wasn't a real smile. Her eyes were flat. I didn't know what that meant, but I knew I didn't want her down. "Let's go. It's late," I said, pulling Alma up, tugging her and Killian along.

We headed back to our cabins, Killian tapping the walls, all perky, as if nothing had ever happened. As if our little conversation were already a thing of the past. Even though it was still fresh on my mind. Even though I still wanted to tell her.

"So do you," I mumbled.

She looked at me quizzically as the three of us ambled down the hall.

"So do you deserve better," Alma clarified my thoughts. She knew. Somehow Alma always knew.

Killian smiled for real this time and bumped her butt with ours. "That's why I love you guys."

DAY 4, 9:10 A.M.
TORTOLA,
BRITISH VIRGIN ISLANDS—

I died and went to heaven. Seriously.

I couldn't believe the exotic painting I stepped into the next morning. Clear blue skies shone above a gleaming white beach and olive mountainside. A searing breeze wrapped around me, inviting my hair to dance and swirl. This. This is how I wanted to wake up every day.

"Where are we?" Yoli mumbled, her sleepy flip-flops brushing the deck.

Alma adjusted her sunglasses. "On the *Temptress*, a cruise ship in the Caribbean?"

"Tortola," I said. I remembered reading the cruise itinerary back in March and wondering why they didn't pick a better port of call. A more popular place people might recognize. I mean, where the heck was Tortola?

But now . . . now I understood why stopping here was a must.

"Virgin Islands," I clarified, unable to tear my eyes away from the curve of the beach.

"Sorry, Killian, you won't be allowed onshore." Alma snickered.

Killian laughed. "Me? All you sluts are staying behind with me."

Monogamous and partway experienced, maybe, but sluts, we were not. Alma and I giggled. And when we did, I felt like the West Indies breeze lifted the sound and carried it out to shore. I turned to see if Yoli was at least smiling. She wasn't. She pretended to be intrigued by a pamphlet.

"Psst," I called.

She looked up and gave me a lame smirk. Was she still mad about last night? She'd seemed fine while we dressed this morning, but now that we were with Killian, she was back to stone. Madame Fortuna would be glad to know she was sort of right. About the strife and the bonds. I hoped that this was as bad as it would ever get.

Hopefully, today would be better. First, we were going to Cane Garden Bay to lie on the beach and do as the tourists do. Then we'd play it by ear, maybe do some shopping, even though I didn't have a whole lot of money to spend. After that, it was anyone's call.

We shuffled down the gangway and waited at a nearby shuttle bus station. Santi and Monica met us there. "Hey, girls. Ready for another wild day?" Santi said, shaking his head.

"We're holding back on the wildness today," Killian said.

I could tell she was determined to keep herself in check. I, however, thought I was being pretty wild compared to my lame self at home. So far, I had had a total stranger rub down my mostly naked body with oil, I'd flirted (at least I thought so) with a hottie named Raul, danced a three-way, and downed three margaritas in a tiny Puerto Rican bar. And we weren't even halfway through the cruise yet.

We took off on the shuttle bus and swirled through the mountain roads until we reached the northern part of the island. Cane Garden Bay was where most boats anchored, since it shielded them from the strongest winds—another thing I'd read from the countless brochures all over the ship. It was a stretch of beach, a white arc that shone alongside the turquoise waters. Even though it was still early, the beach already had its share of tourists finding their spots under the sun.

Santi tipped our driver, then tugged Monica by the hand. I wondered if my parents had ever held hands like that. I couldn't remember. My father left for Seattle, of all places, a long time ago. I always imagined that a handsome man on a horse would one day appear on our front porch and take away my mom and me to live in a house on the beach, but it never happened. Mom seemed to think that maybe Lorenzo was that gallant man in disguise, but my mother can be pretty delusional. Lorenzo burps the alphabet. I would hardly call that gallant.

We scuffled along the sand, looking for a place to drop. There was a perfect spot near a concession stand, but not close enough for people to kick sand all over us.

Yoli shielded her eyes from the sun. "Guys, this place is beautiful." She immediately dropped her bag and started rummaging through it until she found her camera. "Get together."

"Here, I'll take it," Santi said, taking the camera from her.

We stood side by side, the beach and water in the background, my arms wrapped around Yoli and Alma's waists, and Killian's around Alma's, and I could feel one of those moments coming. I tried not to give it too much thought—the mountains, the bay, my friends, young and beautiful in our bikini tops and shorts. One day, we'd look back on this picture after we'd all had our kids and say how skinny we were.

"Say cheese," Monica said next to Santiago.

"Cheeeeeese. . . ."

"Queso," Alma uttered. I laughed out loud. It was going to be a great picture.

After we settled into prime tanning positions, I noticed that a lot of the other beachgoers were passengers from our ship. Over by the concession stand, I even saw Bruno, my older-man, dad's-friend masseur holding hands with the white-dress spa girl.

"Look at my massage guy," I said, and the girls looked. "That's his wife?"

Yoli flopped her hat on top of her head. "Of course.

Didn't you say he was married?"

Killian adjusted her bikini top. "Mm-hm, nice wife."

Yoli, picking up on the sarcasm, defensively said, "It might be his wife!"

Alma nodded. "It might also be his niece."

Killian and I cracked up. I flipped open the lid of my tanning oil. Yoli stuck out her tongue. Who knew? Nobody. So there wasn't any point in racking our brains over it. I chose to believe the spa girl was his wife, who worked on the ship with him, and there they were, having a morning off. On the beach. Holding hands.

I looked at Santi and Monica, the verified married couple in front of us. They lay next to each other but seemed worlds apart. No touching. No kissing. Occasionally, they mumbled something to each other. I looked at Bruno laying a wet one on Spa Girl.

"Okay, so maybe it's not his wife," I said, disappointed.

I wondered where the boys of the *Temptress* were. Raul the Adverb Guy and Tyler-slash-Cute Guy in particular. It wasn't like there was a whole lot to do on Tortola; this beach was pretty much the shining star of the island. Maybe we'd see them. Call me crazy, or maybe just bored, but I was curious to see how the girls would react if Tyler showed up. Would it have been wrong of me to place bets on Killian winning this one?

The sand was superfine, like powdered sugar. And the beach was hot, and getting hotter as the morning went on. I nodded off once, but mostly I thought about how this was my last chance. My last chance to relax before school started.

To be honest, I was proud of myself for having made

it through high school with pretty good grades. I could have made it into many colleges, but I was really excited about the pastry arts program at the French Culinary Institute. When I was accepted, Lorenzo said he didn't feel it was a real school, then he eased up when he realized I could graduate after a year and start making money sooner. Although I love, love, love making desserts, I wasn't thrilled to be joining the workforce three years earlier than my college-bound peers. But what else was I supposed to do? Making desserts is my thing.

When I was little, I used to sit on the kitchen counter and watch my mother make cupcakes for my classmates whenever there would be a school party. She used store-bought cake mixes and frosting, but she would pipe little designs on the tops of each cupcake, sometimes custom-draw something for each of my classmates, and all my friends would ooh and ahh over them. "I wish I had your mom," Killian had told me lots of times over the years. "Mine doesn't even buy cupcakes at the store."

It was really a simple art. Anyone could do it. But no one did. Except my mom, and then me. Yes, I quickly learned that the way into my friends' hearts was through sweet treats. So I started baking cookies, pies, cakes. I would give them away just to see the reactions on people's faces when they'd bite into a shortbread cookie filled with strawberry preserves that I'd made with fresh strawberries from the field by my house. It was relaxing for me to stand in the kitchen and twist, turn, pull, knead dough of all kinds into all different shapes.

So after hearing that chocolatier extraordinaire Jacques Torres taught at the FCI in SoHo, I applied and got in with a scholarship. And I was really, truly happy about that, except . . . I don't know. I just wish I didn't have to start so fast. Considering I wasn't in any hurry to graduate from FCI, I wanted to take a trip with Lorenzo somewhere, just he and I, or maybe even . . . maybe even visit my dad. I don't know.

There were so many things to consider when I got home from the cruise.

"Oh . . . my Lord," I heard Killian say.

"What?" Our heads all came up, but it was hard to see through the sun's glare.

"Tyler."

"Where?" Yoli shielded her eyes.

"Right there, with that chick."

"What chick?" I looked but didn't see them. Oh yeah, now I saw them. In the water. The girl who had been with them last night was in a tiny blue bikini top, which she pressed against Tyler's chest. Her boobs were in direct competition with the surrounding mountains. She and Tyler were stuck together at the lips.

"Slut," Killian said.

"I know. What is she wearing?" I asked.

"Not her. Him."

"Oh." Yes, it was clear that Tyler was on this cruise for one purpose and one purpose only: to be a man-whore. But Killian watched anyway. Because Killian was a voyeur. Or a voyeuse, I guess. And I could tell she wanted to be the one in his arms, instead of Booby Girl, and that this friendship cruise was seriously cramping her style. But I appreciated her efforts to stick with us anyway.

"Well . . ." She sat up and stretched. "Anybody want a drink?"

"I do." I sat up and reached for my little wrap skirt. I'd bought it just before the cruise because I thought it looked cute and islandy.

"Okay, but leave the bedsheet here."

"This isn't a bedsheet, thank you very much. It's a skirt." I wrapped it around my waist.

"Whatever it is."

Alma snorted a laugh. "Bedsheet."

I saw Yoli roll her eyes at us. I narrowed mine at her, like asking what the problem was. She just pursed her lips and shrugged. Yes, okay, this was all a ploy to get Tyler to look at Killian, a check-me-out walk. So what? *Get over it, Yoli. Jesus Christ almighty.* She was acting so juvenile.

Killian touched Santi's shoulder with her toe. "Hey, Santi, how about lending us your presence for a sec, eh?"

Monica shoved her husband awake. Santi looked up. "I don't want any part of it."

But we pouted and pleaded, and Santi was too nice a guy. Monica was one lucky girl. I wondered if she even realized that.

"Fine. Hold on a sec." He stood up and stretched. Let me tell you that for a twenty-seven-year-old guy who was married with a kid, he looked pretty damn good. Which was, of course, stupid to think. It's not like he'd had the baby himself.

Santi walked with us to the concession stand. Killian put her arm on his shoulder. "Don't mind me," she told him.

"What's up your sleeve, little girl?" Santi asked.

She was, of course, kicking it up a notch to get Tyler to notice her. Strutting the sands with an older man and all that. And it was, of course, working. Killian was a pro not to be trifled with. At the concession stand, we asked Santi to *please-please* get some frozen drinks for us, to which he raised a brotherly eyebrow but obliged anyway.

Killian seized the opportunity to readjust her hair clip, letting her blond locks fly around in the breeze. She arched her back ever so slightly, so that her butt stuck out just enough to show off its shape. I watched Tyler and his face-sucker to see if there'd be a reaction. Killian tugged on her bikini bottom. "Oops, wedgie," she said.

"Keep doing that," I said, stealing glances at Tyler and his Latina Barbie doll. "He's looking."

She peeked over her shoulder in a very sexy, but also very bored way. How did she do that? Then she leaned on Santi's shoulder.

"Two for you, two for you . . ." Santi handed us each two frosty beverages. Strawberry or something. I sipped one. Mmm, it felt awesome on my parched tongue.

"Thanks. I know you don't have to do this." Killian spoke into his shoulder.

"You're right. I don't. Enjoy it, 'cause I'm not coming back for round two. Your parents would kill me." He paid the cashier and told him to keep the change.

"Not my parents," Killian said. She jiggled her butt for

good measure to the beat of the calypso music coming from the concession stand radio.

I checked Tyler again. He saw me and grinned. I gave him a finger wave. His girl looked in our direction to see what in the world could possibly be taking away his attention from her investments. She grabbed his chin and planted a kiss on his mouth.

What's the matter? Can't pay attention? I smiled. "Kill, maybe you should go to some acting auditions over the summer," I said.

"Maybe." It was a conversation everyone had had with her at least a dozen times before. *Killian, why don't you go into modeling; you're such a natural. Killian, why don't you become an actress; you could make so much money. . . .* Something. The girl shouldn't let her talent go to waste.

We headed back and passed out the drinks. Killian reached into her bag and tossed a twenty at Santi, which landed on his shoulder while he was lying down again. "For the drinks."

He tossed it back at her. "Save it. You'll need it to post bail."

Killian laughed and put the twenty away.

"I see your boy over there is having a hard time," Alma said, taking a glass, tossing the straw aside. She chugged down half the frosty beverage.

"I'm sure," Killian sang, planting her distraction back down in the sand.

"I can't believe he's with that . . . thing," Yoli said.

Alma lit a long-awaited cigarette and blew out the

smoke with a giant sigh. "At least if he starts drowning, he could use her as a flotation device." Alma. God love her.

We laughed. Where could Raul be? Now *there* was a guy worth fighting over: polite, sweet. But I hadn't seen him since breakfast yesterday. I wanted to see him again. To introduce him to Yoli. That way, both Killian and she could be with someone and shut up.

It was already one o'clock. We were not only buzzed from our drinks, but also red from the sun. And starving. It was a good time to get going, but Killian stood up and said, "Watch this." Words that sent my heart running for cover.

She unknotted the back of her bikini top and plucked it off. Thank goodness Santi and Monica were facedown, baseball caps covering their heads from the sun. "Fee, hold this, please." She dropped the bikini top into my lap and headed for the water.

Every guy around us stopped and focused. The girls did too, but quickly checked their boyfriends' eyes to make sure they were back in the right place. A few whistles pierced the air.

"Killian, what in the world . . ." Yoli shook her head. "There are kids here!"

"So hard-headed, I swear . . ." Alma said, cigarette at her lips.

Yes, Killian definitely liked hearty competition. But I loved her. For doing the things I'd never have the nerve to do. "She's a trip." I smiled.

I watched Tyler in midromp in the water, carrying his

girl. When his eyes froze on the spectacle that was Killian, the girl drooped in his arms. She followed his gaze and saw what he saw. None too happy, Booby Girl stormed out of the water. Just as our golden goddess waded in.

DAY 4, 2:40 P.M.
TORTOLA, BVI—

*T*he Coconut Beach Bar was a grill and hangout in Cane Garden Bay. It was a laid-back place that played reggae music while we had lunch on an outdoor covered deck. I had suggested we eat there after I saw that they served chocolate banana cream pie. I had to see for myself if it was better than mine. Santiago and Monica went shopping, so it was just us girls.

The Caribbean jerk chicken was incredible, although they'd used a few more Scotch bonnet peppers than I would have. Hoo! "Da migh ha may your Top Ten," I told Killian, fanning my tongue with a napkin.

"You think?" She winced and bit into a burger.

"Yeth," I said. Killian's nudie show was definitely one of

her best performances, right up there with teetering off the ship's guard rail à la *Titanic*.

Alma cracked her knuckles. "Daring, yet alluring. Killian's ready for prime time. Right, Yoli?"

Yoli just rolled her eyes, sipping on her water with lemon.

"What did Tyler say when he came up to you?" I asked Killian. We hadn't talked about this while Yoli's brother and sister-in-law were around.

"Nothing. He wanted to see what I was doing later, if I wanted to hang out again."

"Mm-hm," Alma muttered. "'Hang out.'"

Killian slapped Alma's shoulder. "Yes, hang out. You have a problem?"

"None whatsoever," she muttered, picking at her teeth.

"So where are we going from here? We have until six," I said.

Yoli pulled out a pamphlet from her beach bag. "They have something called Dolphin Encounter, where we could swim with the dolphins."

"Tourist crap." Killian sipped from her drink.

"Everything is tourist crap," Yoli said. "We're tourists. So are half the people here."

"True. But I don't think the dolphins would survive Killian," I said with a smile.

Killian looked genuinely hurt. "What would I do to the poor dolphins?"

"You would flash them, for one," Alma said straight into her plate of island BBQ chicken and ribs.

I giggled. "Yes, you might kill them with your heat seekers."

"I do *not* have heat seekers." Killian thumped the table with her hand.

"So does that mean we're not going to see the dolphins, then?" Yoli interjected.

"Those puppies looked pretty alert to me," I continued, but I could see that Yoli was bothered that nobody was listening to her.

Killian jutted out her chest and lifted her boobs with her hands. "They did, didn't they?"

I looked out at the dusty road and saw a girl in a mesh sundress rushing up the steps to our restaurant, clinging to a beach bag, pushing her sunglasses over her knotted hair. I almost didn't recognize her with her chest covered. It was Tyler's Booby Girl. Her friends waited by the road. She went right up to our table and stopped. "Let me tell you something. . . ." She pointed a finger at Killian.

What's this?

"Learn some respect, okay?" She used her hands to accent the *okay*.

Killian leaned back in her seat. "Do I know you?"

"Trust me, you don't want to," Booby Girl threatened.

I checked out Alma's face, midbite of a sparerib, eyes glaring up intently. Uh-oh. *Down, Alma. . . . Easy, girl.* I was very familiar with this look. The first time I saw it was when she was only twelve, two seconds before she charged at her stepfather after he'd yelled at her mom. But so far, except for Grandma Golden Bag in port the other day, she had behaved herself pretty well.

Killian just laughed. Which did not go over well with our intruder.

Booby Girl got close into Killian's face, quickly becoming Psycho Chick. "*Sí*, go ahead and laugh, *puta*, but the next time you pull a trick like that . . . Don't think I'm stupid; I know exactly what you were trying to do—let me tell you, *that* boy is with me!"

"*Puta?*" Alma dropped her sparerib.

Oh, shit.

"Did you just call my friend *puta*, as in slut?"

Oh, shitty shit.

Killian put a hand softly on Alma's arm. "Don't worry about it, sweetie."

"Alma, don't. . . ." I could hear Yoli's voice somewhere in the background. Something about it not being worth it.

Psycho Chick swerved her head a bit and put a hand on her hip. "I wasn't talking to you."

"Okay, listen," I interrupted. "We were having a private lunch here."

"And I was having a private thing with that guy."

"On a public beach?" I knew I was asking for it, but come on, did she not know the definition of *private*?

"Tyler," Killian sang, her face all happy as if there were no hostility here at all.

The girl's eyebrows told us she didn't know who the hell this Tyler person was.

"His name's Tyler." Killian laughed. In her face, I might add. "You didn't even know that, did you?"

Psycho Chick put her nose a millimeter from Killian's

face. "Laugh at me one more time, *come mierda....*" Then she lifted a long-nailed hand and shoved Killian's left shoulder hard enough almost to knock her off the edge of her chair.

Suddenly, Alma was out of her seat, reaching across the table to shove the girl back a few feet. "Take your fake titties and your nasty attitude out of here and hop it back to the ship!"

Holy crap!

One of the girl's friends was suddenly there, tugging on her friend's sleeve. "Let's go. Just leave the stupid bitch alone."

I couldn't believe what I was hearing! Where were these people raised?

"These people" seemed to include Alma, who tossed her chair aside and, I swear, flew at the girls, until Killian and our waiter both tried to get in the middle. It all happened so fast, I couldn't tell what was going on. All I knew was that there was a lot of yelling, and we were going to get kicked out of here for sure.

"Alma!" I yelled. Yoli came over and helped me pry Alma's hands from Psycho Chick's hair. Killian's arm was somewhere between my face and a handful of black locks.

Somehow, the girls managed to free themselves. They backed down the steps. "Just watch out, *puta*, unless you want to get hurt. That's all I'm saying." Psycho Chick spoke between heavy gulps of air. "And keep your bitch on a leash." She spit on the deck. She actually spit on the deck!

Alma surged forward again, but Killian and I had a

pretty good hold on her, so that was the end of that. I looked around and saw that people were watching, but now that it was over, they went back to eating, quietly discussing the lunchtime entertainment.

The reggae music was still playing happily, like nothing had happened.

Our waiter asked if we wanted anything else to drink. I couldn't believe he wasn't kicking us out. "You should have ripped her hair out," he said with a local accent.

"I tried," Alma said, chugging down the rest of her Coke. "But these fools wouldn't let me."

"Well, we didn't want you getting yourself killed," I said, all of a sudden remembering stupid Madame Fortuna again and her stupid prediction. Maybe Killian and I had just succeeded in preventing it from happening. Maybe now we could finally forget about it.

"So you guys are worried about me killing dolphins with my breasts?" Killian snorted. "When Beast here is attacking people?"

"Me?" Alma put a hand to her chest. "You attacked her too!"

"Yeah, but only because you started it."

"She started it!" Alma barked. "Because of your strip-tease! Maybe if you would stop causing problems everywhere we go, Killian, I wouldn't have to defend you all the time."

Killian stared at Alma, not sure if she was kidding or not. It wasn't like Alma to get mad at her. Yoli or me, maybe, but not at Killian. "Well, I never asked for anyone to defend me."

Alma reached into her bag and pulled out yet another

cigarette. She put it to her lips then fished around for her lighter. "You know what? You're right. From now on, you're on your own." The cigarette bobbed up and down as she spoke. She found her lighter, lit it, and breathed in deeply. Definitely stress.

Yoli pulled some cash from her bag and plopped it on the table. She stood up.

"Where are you going?" I asked.

"To the ship."

"Why?"

"Because."

"Because what? Don't listen to them, Yoli."

"Because I'm sick of this. I'm sick of all this fighting!" She scooted past me and stopped when I grabbed her hand.

"So don't fight. Stay. Come on, we're done. Happy-happy, joy-joy. See?" I pushed my face against Killian's. Together we smiled. "Yo, Kill, All, Fee? Forever friends we will be?"

"Quit it, Fiona." Yoli glared at me. "You can be so gullible sometimes," she said, and walked off into the tropical sunshine.

I would have urged her to come back, but she had just called me gullible. Me! Someone ten notches above her when it came to reality checks, but she had the balls to call *me* gullible? I wasn't the one who thought my full-body massage would be rendered with clothes on, or that a guy like Tyler would go for a cutesy, sweet girl like her instead of our resident vixen.

"Pfft. Whatever," I said.

"Ouch."

I eyed Killian. This was all her fault, but I wasn't going to tell her and ruin our day even more. "Shut up," I said, and for good measure, added, "*puta*." I tried to contain my smile.

Killian's rolled into a laugh. "Make me, bitch."

And then Alma laughed hard, smoke curling out of her nose like a fire-breathing dragon, so I let it go. Because if Alma laughed, then I knew we were okay.

DAY 4, 4:30 P.M.
TORTOLA, BVI—

*A*fter we left the grill, I kicked myself in the butt for not having tried the chocolate banana pie, our whole reason for going there. Amid the excitement, we'd forgotten to order it.

We stood in the middle of a shopping district, unable to decide between the Dolphin Encounter and snorkeling, so we ended up hitting the stores instead. The dolphin thing would have been cool, but Yoli had already returned to the ship, and it was her idea to begin with. We'd have to come back next year. Maybe we could do this every summer as a tradition. But without the street fight.

Plus Killian "really, really, really" needed to buy herself

something after the *puta* incident. So we entered a jewelry store where the people behind the counter stared at us like in that movie with Julia Roberts where she's a hooker with a lot of money to spend. I didn't know why they were looking at us like that, because Killian had some serious cash to drop.

She made the lady take out practically every pair of earrings in the store, then put them all back. I knew she was doing it to be a pain in the ass because of the way they were examining us. Then she asked the clerk to take out some bracelets with pretty blue stones on them.

"What is that?" Killian asked the woman, who was probably starting to wonder if we were going to buy something or not.

"Larimar. It's native to the Caribbean."

"Larimar?" Killian repeated.

The woman gave her a vacant stare.

"It's beautiful," I said.

"It's a hook bracelet," the salesperson explained. "If you wear the hook facing your heart, then your heart is taken and good fortune will come your way. If you wear it away from your heart, you're available."

"Without good fortune?" I asked.

"With good fortune."

Killian and I looked at each other, impressed. "We could definitely use some good fortune," she said. "How much?"

It was pretty expensive for just one bracelet, so imagine my eyes when Killian asked for four of them to be wrapped in little boxes with bows. The salesperson was highly surprised, especially when Killian's credit card matched her ID and the transaction went through without a hitch.

"Killian, what are you doing?" I asked.

"I just wanted to buy you guys something for graduation."

Outside the store I gave Killian a big hug and took out my new bracelet. "Thank you, *chica*."

"Yeah, man, thanks." Alma kissed Killian's cheek and tried hers on.

It was really pretty. I made sure to wear it with the hook facing toward my heart. Killian and Alma faced theirs away. "Maybe that will change by the end of the cruise," Killian said.

"Come on, you said Tyler was a jerk."

"I didn't mean Tyler. I meant anybody. But Tyler is a cutie. Woof, is he a cutie."

"Yes, okay, we know!" I said. God! Who cared about him anymore?

We drifted in and out of shops along the street. There were lots of beautiful skirts and dresses, but it was all stuff I could get at home. Miami had a lot of the same clothes. I felt like I had to buy Killian something in return, but my cash had to last through the end of the cruise. Besides, Killian didn't need anything I could afford to buy her anyway.

Killian sighed and fingered a scarf hanging on a big wooden ring. What was up with her? "You guys swear not to tell Yoli?"

Some local kids screamed as they ran past us. Alma

gasped. "You did him."

Killian tried to look offended. "I told you I didn't, Alma dear. Why would I lie?"

"Then what?" I asked, touching my bracelet, feeling the smoothness of the larimar stone.

Killian plucked the scarf off the ring and tried it on around her neck. "Tyler and them?"

"Uh-huh . . . ?" She couldn't have divulged her info any slower.

"You thought I was crazy? Those guys are worse. They do this cruise every year after finals and have messed-up parties in their rooms like every night."

"Messed-up?" I asked. Did I really want to know?

"Yep."

"So they're in college?" Alma said, getting her facts straight.

Killian laughed sarcastically. "Yeah. And they're all alkies too. If you can think it, they drink it. Plus Tyler's got all kinds of . . . stuff."

"Drugs," I guessed, a little too loud.

Killian's hands stopped in their tracks, and she eyed me. "Louder, Fiona, so everyone can hear."

"Sorry." I winced. "Tell me you didn't do any of that the other night."

Killian rearranged the scarf and shrugged. "Like I need any of that to be high."

"True," Alma said, watching a tall, elegant man walk by. "The world is your drug."

"Exactly." Killian tried to see herself in a blurry mirror tacked onto a wooden column. "Does this make me look like an old lady?"

"Yes," Alma and I said together. Killian pulled off the scarf and put it back on the ring.

We left the store and slowly walked in the direction of the bus stop. "So you just hung out with them, nothing else?" I asked. If I chipped at her enough times, eventually the truth would come out.

"I had a few beers with them in the room," she said. "But that was it, I swear. I just watched them for the longest time. It was funny. They're bad . . . like *really* bad. They had girls there all night, going in and out of rooms, closing doors and stuff. One of them was running around with a whipped cream bikini on." She laughed. "She went into the bathroom with one of Tyler's buddies, and you know those bathrooms, how tiny they are!"

"So you lied!" I flounced in place. *Aha!*

Killian smiled. "It's no big deal. I was only there for a little while."

"So they have wild parties in their rooms," I reiterated, trying to imagine the frat boy scenario in my head. Seemed normal, I guess. I'd seen it in movies enough times.

Killian's eyes opened wide. "Yeah, except they're all players. They're on this quest to get with as many girls as they can. To see who ends up sleeping with the most."

"How would you know? If you're one of the girls they're after, I mean," Alma asked.

Killian did a little butt shake. "Takes one to know one." She chuckled.

"Fabulous." Alma blew out a staccato snort. "So they're having pimp wars."

I doubted anyone ever had pimp wars over at the French Culinary Institute, and I was definitely glad no one was playing me. These were college situations I'd definitely be missing out on. Which was fine. I was never one to be making merry with pimps anyway. But this was right up Killian's alley.

Well, a bit of a shocker, but it could've been worse. I suppose they could've been sex-slave scouts looking to abduct a few American teens to take back to faraway countries. Then again, if they were, would they advertise it? Normally, I'd shrug off that kind of thought as neurotic, but there was that whole prediction issue to watch out for, so my stomach did a flip. We should stay away from those guys. Just in case.

Alma fished around in her purse for another cigarette. She had to take advantage of the shore leave. "So, last time we'll ask . . . Did you do the deed with him?"

Killian scoffed. "No! Why won't anyone believe me? Yes, Tyler definitely tried to get with me at first, but when he saw he was wasting precious game time, he quit trying."

We gave her doubtful stares.

"I swear!"

"Then why can't we tell Yoli?" I asked.

"Go ahead if you want, but I don't think we should. She's on that mission to do something wild, and telling her might drive her to it." Killian sounded a bit too mama hen–ish herself.

"Yeah, but shouldn't we let Yoli decide that for herself?" I asked. "I mean, she *is* a big girl. Plus Madame Fortuna—"

"*Ay*, please!" Alma interrupted. "Enough with Madame *Fart*una already."

Killian laughed. "I know, right? Nothing's going to happen to us, Fiona. It would've happened already. Don't envision problems where there aren't any."

"I'm not." My tone sounded defensive, but was that true? Was I now imagining things because of the tarot reading?

We came to the end of the shopping district. I thought the conversation might be over, but then Killian had that faraway look of hers again. Something was brewing. "Listen. . . ." she said, watching some kids have a pebble-throwing contest in the sand. "Yoli saved me once."

Alma chuckled. "Killian, we were kids. You weren't really going to fly off the Himalaya at the fair. You know that, right?"

Killian's eyes were focused. "Whether I was or not, doesn't matter. The point is, she thought she was saving me. And that was more than anyone did for me at the time. So I owe her one, you know?" She turned a sad smile toward me.

I nodded. Yeah, I always knew Killian felt grateful for that. But still, maybe it was just better to tell Yoli straight out. However, Killian could be right: The new Yoli might find Tyler's antics even more appealing.

We crossed the street and walked along the beach wall for a while. The sun started its early-evening descent. The sky was still blue, but the sides of the buildings were bright orange. "Anyway," Killian added, "Tyler and his friend Edgar—"

"Allan Poe?" Alma said.

"Seriously." I laughed. "Who's named Edgar anymore? You mean the ugly guy?"

"He's not that ugly. Well, anyway, they want to start a production company in the future, like that guy did with *Girls Gone Wild*? And he told me that I could be in their first film."

Alma scuffed some gravel with her sandal. "Tell me you didn't fall for that."

Killian grinned. "I know he was trying out a line, but you never know, maybe they will. And it might be a good way to get noticed, like if I ever went into acting."

I hated when Killian talked this way. She was smarter than this, but sometimes, for some reason, the dumbest crap came out of her mouth. "You think talent agents are going to care that your wet T-shirt starred in a low-budget film? You'd be killing your career before it even got started."

"Fee, a lot of actresses do stuff like that before making it big. Forget it, I shouldn't have said anything to you."

Then I felt bad. If I acted like a mother hen, I'd be treated as one. The only way to get through to Killian was to make her feel it was okay to tell me. "Sorry, just . . . Go on."

She eyed me sideways and made that frying-egg sound she loved so much. "I'm not saying I'm going to do it. I'm just saying it might be fun."

"'Fun,'" I repeated. I just couldn't believe her, yet it shouldn't have surprised me.

"Yes, Fiona . . . fun. Did it ever occur to you that I might want to have a relationship one day, that I might want to get married and have kids? That this is the only time in my life when I might get to act spontaneous?"

Great. Killian wanted to star in a college boy's home videos. A perfectly smart, capable girl keeping herself down. Suddenly, I wanted to head back to the ship. Find Yoli. Someone halfway sane to talk to.

"Anyway, I'm not doing it," she said, stretching her long torso. "Even though the offer still stands. I only wanted you to know what those guys are up to."

"Well, they sound like nice boys," Alma said in an old lady voice. "Just loverly."

Fine. So I was a bit disappointed. I couldn't imagine Killian, who was interesting enough for a bona fide Hollywood film, involved in that crap, even if it was for the sole purpose of being spontaneous. Why she felt the need to rebel was a mystery to me. I know her parents weren't the most nurturing of folks, but it's not like they were never there. Actually . . . they weren't. Never mind. Me, the craziest thing I would do on this cruise was maybe kiss someone else.

Bad, Fiona! Why would you even think that?

Suddenly I felt guilty for not missing Lorenzo enough. During the whole trip back through the winding mountain roads, I tried to ignore the feeling. But I kept playing with my hook bracelet. Away: heart available.

Toward: heart taken.

Away.

Toward.

Away.

Toward.

For a minute, I left it at away. Just to see what it would look like.

DAY 4, 6:28 P.M.
AT SEA—

*M*y head wanted to crash into a pillow, but I didn't come on this cruise to sleep. So I forced myself to sit up and look around the cabin. Whether I liked it or not, I was going back out there to search for Yoli, or hang by myself in the movie theater. This was too weird a day not to forget about it somehow. Besides, it couldn't get worse, could it?

Scratch that.

I took a cool shower in the teeny stall, then slathered aloe vera lotion all over my body. *Hello, mirror.* Hmm, a killer tan should be showcased with a killer outfit. I rummaged through Yoli's drawers and threw on her solid green minidress with the tiny flowers along the hem. It was a little shorter on me than it was on her, on account of my being four inches taller, but it accented the new olive color of my skin. If Lorenzo saw me in it, he'd freak.

Lorenzo. I remembered my hook bracelet and turned it toward my heart. Even though he can be a butthead.

The *Temptress* was leaving Tortola behind. I was sad to see it go, getting smaller as we moved out to sea. On the upper deck, there were tons of people facing the island, like they'd miss it too. When I got a better look, I noticed they were watching the sunset: a fiery orange ball descending behind the mountains. The sky, red and pink, and purple in the east. An art gallery in the clouds.

"Have you ever seen anything so beautiful?"

I turned around, startled.

Raul.

He laughed, hands in his pants pockets. "I'm sorry. That came out way cornier than intended." His eyes fell on the sunset, his face and white billowed shirt aglow in orange light. I tried not to picture him as the strapping, royalty-in-disguise hunk on the illustrated cover of a romance novel.

"Yeah, it did," I said, smiling a little too big for someone with a boyfriend.

"Sorry 'bout that." He looked down, then back at me. "But it is, right?"

All I saw were great teeth, dimples, sexy honey brown eyes. "Is what?" I asked, because morons lose track of small talk easily.

"The sunset." His eyes twinkled. I didn't know eyes could

actually twinkle. I felt like someone had slapped me over the head with a My Little Pony. *Think straight, Fee.*

"Yes, it's incredible." Should I keep talking to him? Wouldn't that be like cheating on Lorenzo? God, that sounded lame even in my own head. *Of course not. I can just talk to the guy.*

"Where are your friends?" he asked.

"Oh, uh, actually, I don't know." I glanced around, hoping maybe I would see one of them. This was one of those moments they would never believe unless they saw if for themselves. Like catching the biggest fish in the sea then letting it go. *"Sure, Fiona. Sure you talked to Raul the Adverb Guy in front of a gorgeous sunset."* "We spent the day together. But we're taking a break."

He nodded. "I know what you mean. I'm here with my cousins."

"Ah."

"After a while with them, it gets . . ." He paused.

"Tedious?"

He looked at me curiously. "Yeah, tedious. Good word."

I smiled at the compliment, but why did I say that? These were my girls, my friends, who I'd pillage and plunder for. And I just called them tedious?

I swept my hair out of my eyes. "I didn't mean it like that. It's just . . . they're all antsy lately and at each other's throats."

"Friends do that sometimes. Sounds normal to me."

I guess he was right. I liked that I could talk to him and not feel like he was trying to hook me in or smooth talk me in any way. Except for that sunset thing.

"Am I bothering you? I can leave you alone if you want."
He gestured away.

"No, no. . . ."

"You were completely amazed with the view so I wanted
to say something."

"Oh, I know. It's gorgeous. I mean, I never see sunsets
like this in Miami. Or maybe I just never go outside to see
them even though they're always there."

"You're from Miami?" he asked.

"Yeah. And you?"

"Orlando, originally. But I'm graduating from
Gainesville next year."

"Ah," I said. He was a UF Gator. Yoli was going to be
a Seminole. So much for thinking he could be a good
match for Yoli. It would never work between them. Oh,
well.

"You want to sit down?" He pulled up a lounge chair.
Actually, it would be nice to sit. I was tired, but I still wanted
to enjoy the rest of the evening.

"Thanks." I sat down. He did too, on the end of my
chair, since all the other chairs were taken. I laid my head
back and sighed. It was quickly turning into a spectacular
night. Where the sky was purple, some stars were already
beginning to peek out. Plus this gorgeous man kept talking
to me. Maybe I was hallucinating.

"What do you do in Miami?" he asked.

"Oh, uh . . . I just graduated."

"From where?" He looked interested. Too interested. He

thought I meant college, didn't he?

"Bay High." And since it didn't seem to register in his head right away, I clarified. "High school."

"Oh." For a second, a look of disappointment flitted across his face.

"But I'm eighteen!" I thought of adding, just in case he wanted maybe to kiss me or get my number for when this cruise was over. And . . . *Why* was I thinking these things?

"So what are your plans now?"

See, now we were talking. Plans, I knew. My life was all about plans. "Well . . ."

I told him all about the pastry arts program. How I was really excited about it, but that I didn't want to be graduating so quickly because it'd mean starting to work all the earlier, but how my mother really wanted it because she had had to work so hard as a single mom, and this way, I would have it made in the shade.

"Wow, sounds awesome. So well thought out," he said, nodding.

"Thanks." *I think.* I played with my hook bracelet, opening and closing it. Didn't mention Lorenzo.

"I know exactly what you mean about not starting right away." He leaned forward, hands clasped between his knees. "I'm graduating next year, but I want to travel for a while before starting my career. Maybe start earning paychecks a year after that. Work will still be there, ready and waiting."

"Exactly!" I said. Wow. He got it. My life was ready and waiting too! "What do you do?" It felt strange having this conversation. So adult. I would never have in a million years asked my guy friends at Bay High what they *did*.

"You mean, what am I studying?" He raised his eyebrows.

God, I was hopeless. "Yes, that's what I meant."

"I'm studying to be a systems analyst."

Okay, I didn't know what that was exactly, but it sounded boring. I bet this cruise was doing him good. I nodded like I knew exactly what he was talking about.

"I also do some freelance work on the side," he said, looking at his cousins, who gave us the occasional curious glance. "With them."

"Ah." Again, I didn't know what kind of freelance work, and I felt too stupid to ask, like I was supposed to know what he was talking about. "Where are you thinking of traveling next year?"

He leaned back and thought about it. There was a spark in his eyes I can't describe, like his possibilities were endless. All I know is that it sent a shot of adrenaline running through me I didn't expect. "Rome maybe? London, Paris, Cairo, all those cities, you name it. I want to see cathedrals, opera houses, castles, pyramids, ruins my dad always told me about."

Wow. Wandering the world, free of responsibility, no work, no school, just experiencing life. So bohemian. I could never live that way. I'd feel I was taking advantage of my mom's generosity or something. Besides, I couldn't just leave Lorenzo in the dust. Still, it couldn't hurt to wonder what would happen if we put our relationship on hold, just for a year.

Forget it; it would never happen, even though I was

thinking about it. Which was new for me. Why was I always so afraid to fantasize about things, even if they never happened? Like what was my big deal in talking to Raul? What was wrong with having a friendly conversation? Nothing. I could daydream, couldn't I? That I was on this cruise single, that we'd have a great dinner then a few drinks and get all giddy with each other, and then . . .

I caught sight of Yoli coming out of the double doors, walking with—you'll never guess. Okay, guess. Tyler. And Edgar Allen Poe. And the other cute guy from the port.

"Isn't that your friend?" Raul asked. Observant, I must say. Hmmm, his eyes had lingered over Yoli at breakfast yesterday too.

"Yeah. She's great," I said, just to plant the idea in Raul's head since I couldn't have him for myself. "Do you mind if I go talk to her? I haven't seen her since this afternoon."

I could always see Yoli later in our cabin, but I wanted to know what she was doing with Tyler. Besides, I wanted her to know the full truth about those guys, regardless of what Killian said. Just so she wouldn't get involved.

"By all means." Raul smiled, full dimples and all. "See you later."

I got up and tugged down on my dress. Yoli's dress. "Hopefully," I said. Great, so now I was Adverb *Girl*. He smiled again. He had to stop doing that, or he would destroy me.

Yoli and Tyler were leaning against the railing, facing the ocean. The other guys had spread out, so they were talking alone. I debated interrupting, but went for it anyway. It's not like they were making out or anything. Tyler was holding a cup of what looked like Coke.

I touched Yoli's arm. "Hey," I said, out of breath.

She turned around and acted all fake-surprised. "Fee! This is my friend Fee," Yoli told Tyler.

"Yeah, I remember." Tyler leaned back to get a better look at me. *Don't even think about it, Slickness.* "Princess Fiona, right?"

You know, with a running start, I could so easily have pushed him over that guard rail. But I decided to let him live. "Man, you're hilarious." I smiled.

He smiled too. Either he was clueless or just so used to having girls fawn all over him that he didn't notice sarcasm when he heard it. His eyes looked a little watery, and maybe it was me, but his speech was just a tad slow. I guess his Coke was more like a Happy Coke. Killian's description of him and his friends as alkies flitted through my head.

"Can I talk to you a second?" I asked Yoli.

She obviously did not appreciate my attempt to thwart her plan of finally attaining Tyler Status. "Can we talk *later*?"

Telling her that Cute Guy was now Party Hardy Frat Guy would have to wait, it seemed. Then again, if I told her, he just might become more desirable to her, now that she was all *I'm-going-to-do-something-crazy-on-this-cruise.* Maybe Killian was right. I didn't know what to do. My brain hurt.

I feigned a reason to stick around two seconds more.

"Have you seen Alma?"

"Nooo." Anyone could've seen the laser beams that came out of Yoli's eyes just then.

Of course she hadn't seen Alma. Why, she was wandering the ship with drunk subhumans who considered bouncing quarters into tiny glasses an amusing pastime, not having fun with her friends like she was supposed to. I looked at Tyler and tried to push away images of him playing Naked Twister with ten sorority girls.

I sent Yoli secret messages with my eyebrows. "Well, will you help me look for her in a while?" *Just leave him Yoli. . . . Come with me.*

"Fee, I'll meet you in the dining room in a bit." Her ESP receptors were obviously set to Off.

"All right, see you there." I pointed to an invisible watch on my wrist, reminding me of my mother for some reason. There was Yoli, finally having her cake and eating it too—a minivictory over Killian the Man Charmer—and I was trying to ruin it. But worrying about her was kind of stupid, because it wasn't like she was really going to drink or drug herself silly when she felt self-conscious about removing her clothing at the spa. I mean, come on!

I walked away from them, smiling to myself. Why was I worrying about Yoli? She would never go too far.

Then I remembered what Killian had told us about Tyler. Yoli might not take things too far, but if she was under Tyler's spell . . .

I stopped smiling. I knew it was dumb, but I got chills. For a moment, I couldn't be sure about anything, especially Tyler. In my head, I could hear Killian and Alma telling me that I was imagining problems where there were none, but instincts were instincts for a reason. I saw that on *Oprah* once.

Damn you, Madame Fortuna, for screwing with my head.

DAY 4, 8:35 P.M.
AT SEA—

$\mathcal{S}$ ome friendship cruise this was turning out to be. Killian and Alma were nowhere to be found. Yoli had disappeared too. I ended up having dinner with Santi and Monica, who had probably been hoping to have a nice romantic dinner by themselves. Either that or private arguing time. But the key lime pie was yum-yum *superb*! I loved that word when I read it in restaurant guides. Hopefully, a food critic would one day use it to describe a creation of mine: "Superb, O pastry chef Fiona!"

"So . . ." Monica twiddled her thumbs and occasionally glanced at Santiago. She probably felt sorry for me, having lost all my friends to sun coma or whatever else could be occupying their time. "You must be thrilled about going to New York."

It took all my power not to lick my plate clean. "Oh, yeah. Totally."

"You're not thrilled, are you?" Her smile dampened.

"Yes!" I put down my fork gingerly to abate my piglike behavior. "It's been a dream of mine since I was a little kid."

"It's true." Santi sighed. "I remember all those cookies you used to bake me every year for my birthday." He smiled.

I felt myself blush. Yes, I remembered that, too. I remembered that Yoli's cute older brother had a fondness for peanut butter chocolate chip. March 28. And every year I was happy to provide him with the saturated fats for which his body longed.

"When am I going to get more?" He laughed.

Monica pushed a finger into his side. "We don't need any more."

That was the downside of making desserts nowadays. It was a dying art. When I was a kid, everyone loved them. Now, everybody was on some diet. Why couldn't they just eat one cookie and call it a day? Why was it craziness or nothing?

"Anytime you want. I'll ship them from school," I offered.

"What's Lorenzo going to do without your desserts for a whole year?" Santi asked.

Monica sucked in a breath. "Honey! What's Lorenzo going to do without *Fiona* for a whole year? Who cares about desserts?" She gave me a sisterly look. "Can you believe him?"

"I know what he meant." I smiled.

Work for his dad, that's what Lorenzo would do. I didn't like that he wasn't going to college for now, but since his dad was so certain Lorenzo would be running the family business one day, Lorenzo had postponed it. Fend off the girls knocking on his door, 24-7, that's another thing he'd do. I hated having to contend with all his mom's friends' daughters, poseurs hoping to be Mrs. Lorenzo Peralta. Not that Lorenzo paid any attention to them. I knew he wanted to be with me and no one else. Even though I had found those messages in his Sent folder those couple of times, but it had never happened again.

I was glad Monica wasn't going on about long-distance relationships and how they never work out, the way Killian and Alma always told me. I guess because she and Santi were high school sweethearts too, she knew what I was facing. "I'm sure he'll visit you, you'll see," Monica assured me.

"Oh, he will. He plans on coming up once a month. Anyway, it's only for a year."

She gave me a sympathetic smile and sipped her cappuccino. Why was she giving me those sorry looks? Don't tell me she didn't like Lorenzo either.

I stole glances at the two of them having their coffee in silence, watching the people parade in the dining room. Is that what Lorenzo and I would look like in a few years? After we'd had our first baby? They didn't look bored with each other. But they didn't look ecstatically happy either. As a married couple, I guess you could say they were comfortable. Just . . . there.

❧ ❧ ❧

A loud knock ripped me from my sleep. In my dreams, I was in a prison cell, banging on the iron bars to be let out. It was me who was knocking. Wasn't it? I turned and looked out my barred-up window to see a huge ocean liner half up in the air, sinking into the depths of the ocean. It was horrifying. Were Killian, Alma, and Yoli on it? I heaved into the toilet next to me. "One of you will not come home," I heard an old prison guard woman croak. Then she laughed, her teeth rotten. Her eyes, yellow!

I heard the knock again. What? Who? I sat up and rubbed my eyes, disoriented. "Leave me alone!" I half mumbled, half yelled. Where was I? In the darkness of the room, I quickly realized I was in my cabin on a fun cruise, not in a prison, and that Yoli was underneath her comforter, snoring.

I glanced at the clock. 8:00 A.M. Oh, thank you God, it was only a dream. My friends were not plunging into the sea.

Another loud knock. "Hold on!" I cried. *Geez.* I stumbled out of bed, tripping on the clothes Yoli had left on the floor. When did she come in? I couldn't even remember.

I unlocked the door, cracking it open. It was Killian, all perky and ready to go. "You guys are still sleeping? Come on! We're in St. Thomas!"

"Huh?"

She laughed. Behind her, Alma closed their cabin door shut. They were both dressed in shorts and tanks, their hair tied up, ready for another blazing day. "Is Yoli there?" Killian whispered.

"Yes, where else would she be?" I mumbled.

"With Tyler?"

My eyes sprang open and I looked at Yoli's bed. A deep snore emerged from underneath the heavily patterned covers. "What do you mean *with*?" Last I saw Yoli, she was hanging out on the upper deck with him. But Killian had said with like . . . *with*.

Killian and Alma looked at each other, then at me. "We saw them at the Bora Bora after dinner," Killian whispered, "dancing. So maybe she's in a better mood."

"Dinner where? *I* was at dinner. I didn't see you two."

Killian shrugged. "Pizza bar. We tried to find you." Killian couldn't convince a baby with that lame excuse. I knew she'd wanted to break away with fellow *loca* Alma for a while.

"Well, you must not've looked very hard. I was in the dining room. Same time, same place." *Abandoned. Discarded.*

She glanced sheepishly at her nails. "Are you going to get dressed or what? Lord, you're a mess, Fiona." She reached out and tried combing my hair with her fingers, but they got stuck.

I must have slept like a rock, because all I remember was coming back after dinner with Santi and Monica and crashing. Yoli hadn't come in yet. "So they went dancing?" I whispered.

Alma raised an eyebrow. "Uh-huh. . . ."

"You don't think they . . ." I wasn't going to say it with Yoli right there. She'd better not have. She'd just better not have.

"We don't know. Let's wake her up," Killian said, pushing

me out of the way. She went right over to Yoli's bed and sat at the edge. "Good morning, my little pumpkin. How was your night?"

Could Yoli have really spent half the night with Tyler?

Yoli wriggled around on her bed but basically stayed asleep.

"Wakey, wakey. . . ." Killian cooed.

"Mmhhnn," Yoli groaned.

Alma leaned in the doorway and watched impatiently.

Finally Killian just let her have it. "Yoli, what happened last night? Did you screw him?"

"Kill!" I blurted. She could be so blunt sometimes, it bordered on insensitive. "Leave her alone."

Alma shook her head.

"Sorry, Yoli. I meant, did you rolli in the polli with Tyler's cannoli?"

"What the hell is that?" I tried suppressing a laugh. If I were Yoli, I'd be pissed if Killian tried waking *me* up with this barrage of questions.

Then, it was like the possessed little girl from *The Exorcist* was suddenly with us in the room. Yoli sat up and focused on Killian, her eyes little slits. "You are such a bitch, you know that?" She breathed in Killian's face what must have been the raunchiest morning breath, because Killian scooted back an inch and nearly fell off the bed.

A moment of sticky silence hung like flypaper. Even Killian didn't know what to say. I looked at Alma. Her eyes were wide, wide open. It was probably time to clear the room. Mount Yoli was about to blow, and we were without our lava boats.

"I can't believe you come in here to wake me up, and all you want to know is whether I slept with Tyler or not."

"Well, did you?"

"Killian!" I said. "God!"

Yoli threw herself back down like a pissed-off four-year-old. "Go to hell," she mumbled.

Killian put her hand where Yoli's hip might be under the covers. "Yoli, I was just—"

"Leave me the fuck alone."

Wheeze! Yoli? *Using the F word?*

"Who are you and what have you done with Yoli?" Killian tried to pull the covers off her. It was so funny, but intrusive at the same time, I didn't know if I wanted to laugh or slap Killian.

"Kill, stop," I said, pointing to the doorway. "Just go, please? We'll meet you at breakfast, all right?"

But Killian was on a mission. "Hello? My little crazy cruiser?"

"Killian, stop!" Even though I'd never seen Yoli hit anybody, I thought now would be a good time if she wanted to.

"All right, fine." Killian got up and straightened her jean shorts. "See what you can get out of her," she said to me.

"You see?" Yoli sat right back up. "That's exactly what's wrong with you! You think everything is so damn funny, everything's such a joke, ha, ha!"

Killian made an annoyed sound and started leaving. "Whatever."

"Where are you going? I'm talking to you." It was hard to take Yoli seriously with all those curly locks from her sleep ponytail falling into her face.

Killian turned back to her. "You just told me to leave you alone. Which is it, Yoli? I'm not good with contradictions."

Yoli yanked off the covers and charged toward the bathroom, mostly for change of position, I think. She turned and stood there glaring at Killian. "You know what? Forget it." She started positioning and repositioning the bathroom items around the sink, making herself look more neurotic than menacing.

Killian put a hand on her hip. "Why are you being such a baby? You wanted me to back off the guy, and I did. Now you're pissed because I'm asking how it went?"

"I'm pissed because you're trivializing this whole thing. I'm your source of entertainment. You always do that. Well, I'm sorry if sex is a joke to you, but it's not to me."

"I never said it was. I was just trying to have fun. This is supposed to be a *fun* trip. Fun, fun . . . see? Say it with me," Killian chided.

"Look. . . ." Yoli breathed out a forceful sigh. "When I came back to the ship yesterday, when you three stayed behind and did whatever you did without me . . ."

I checked out the floor. Well, I'm sorry we had a good time without her, but I'd tried to stop her from leaving. She didn't want to stay.

Yoli went on. "He came up to me and started talking to me. Not you, not anybody else. Me." She pointed to herself, because I guess we needed help knowing what "me" meant.

Killian sighed and laughed at the same time. "That's because—"

"No," I said too quickly, giving Killian a sharp look. I

knew where she was going with this. And I did *not* want Yoli thinking that Tyler was only with her for his own purposes. Give the poor girl a break!

Yoli scrunched her eyebrows together at me. "'No' what?"

"No because you shouldn't spend any more time with him, Yoli. Remember that crazy girl at lunch yesterday, that psycho boob chick? She said to stay away from him." Yes, that was good. That was definitely good. It was a matter of safety. Safety was of utmost importance.

"Finish what you were saying," Yoli said to Kill, who was turning around to leave. "'That's because' what?"

"Nothing. Because nothing. Just . . . go and do whatever. I'm over this shit."

"No kidding," Alma said, then looked at me. "Coming, Fee?"

Even I was sick of this crap already. Madame Fortuna was right about the storms and strife. I just didn't think they were going to happen indoors. "I'll find you guys," I said, watching them march away down the hall.

"She's being such a wench," Yoli said when we were alone. "Right?"

I looked at her standing there all victorious like she'd just won some battle, when what she'd really succeeded in doing was putting up a barricade between her and Killian, and Alma, and maybe even me. I wanted to tell her that she was wrong, that she'd been wrong from the very first moment she laid eyes on that guy. I wanted to tell her that she was wrong about Killian too. That in her own weird way, Kill was trying to protect her. But she was being impossible.

"Fiona?"

I couldn't say it. Instead, "I talked to that guy Raul yesterday. He's really nice. If you want to do something spontaneous, do it with him." Even though I wished he was mine, all mine, but I knew that wouldn't happen.

She looked confused. "Adverb Guy?" She gave a short laugh and leaned over the sink with her toothbrush. "He's cute, but I don't want a nice guy."

Now I was really glad I hadn't told her the truth about Tyler. It would've heightened the appeal factor for sure. Instead, here's what would happen: Yoli would find him somewhere today with another girl making out, like with that girl on the beach, and hopefully she'd forget about him. The problem would solve itself.

"Why not, Yoli?" I asked. "It's weird; you're acting like Killian. It doesn't suit you."

"I am not!" she spat. "I'm just tired of everyone thinking I'm still a little girl, when I'm not."

I loved how she had to assert that last piece like I wasn't aware. "Okay," I said. "So can't you change your image with someone else? You and Killian are ruining our trip."

Yoli's eyes opened up. Her mouth looked like it wanted to say something profound, but all that came out was, "*Ock*. Thanks, Fee."

Silence.

Nail picking.

Finally Yoli said, "Look, I know you think Tyler's an ass, but he isn't. He was being really sweet to me, and I want to see him again."

Well, then it was in fate's hands. The problem was . . .

we all had had a glimpse of fate at the fair the other night. And as much as Yoli was acting all multiple personality, I wanted her to come home safe.

I closed the door and searched the drawers for something to wear. I didn't know what there was to do in St. Thomas, but I knew one thing: I was sick of all this so I was going out alone.

DAY 5, 10:00 A.M.
ST. THOMAS, U.S. VIRGIN ISLANDS—

*Y*oli wasn't happy about it, but at that point, I didn't care anymore. If Killian and Yoli wanted to waste our last weeks together arguing over some clown, that was up to them. I would've tried to keep things from turning into World War III between them, but this was our last port of call, and I didn't know when I might take another trip again. I wanted to enjoy myself while I still could. Like Raul said.

I stopped at the ship's information desk to get an idea of what there was to do in Charlotte Amalie, the main port of St. Thomas. A woman behind the desk, who looked vaguely like my mother, gave me some suggestions and handed me lots of reading material. I only heard every other word she said. I was too busy thinking of Mom and what she might be doing right now, like planting basil seeds, having her overripe mango smoothie, or calling into the office to see what the work landscape looked like before wandering in at noon.

I thanked the woman and followed the light at the end of the tunnel to the outside world. A gust of hot wind warmed my face; the bright sunshine immediately made me smile. I really didn't think that anything could have been more beautiful than Tortola, but St. Thomas was quickly climbing the ranks. At the bottom of the steps, a steel drum band played a Beatles song. One of the younger drummers smiled at me as I walked by. I smiled back.

The lady had told me to take any one of the taxis waiting outside. *Eenie-meenie-miney-moe* . . . I picked a nice white one, strolling up to the driver, who was leaning against his car.

"Good morning, miss," he said, folding a newspaper and putting it under his arm. "Where are you off to today?"

I checked the brochures, trying to remember what the woman had told me. "Up the mountain, to see the view, then into town." From there, I'd find another taxi to take me to Coral World, one of St. Thomas's biggest attractions.

"Shopping, shopping," he sang, opening the back door of the cab for me.

You could tell the guy was comfortable in his driver's seat, with all his papers, pens, photos, beads, and whatnots. When he took off, I almost had a coronary when I noticed we were on the opposite side of the road. Leave it to me to pick the driver most likely to crash into a mountain. So the one not coming home was me, I guess, due to fiery collision against oncoming car in St. Thomas. My last moments spent with a hapless local. But then I remembered that these islands used to be British, so everyone drove on the left side.

Whew! Stress is a funny thing.

My driver didn't talk much, which was good. I never did like conversations with strangers, though I'd better get used to it, going to New York and all. Plus, this was my first time exploring a city without my mother or friends, so I didn't want anything distracting me from remembering my way back to the ship. The man just hummed along to an eighties song on the radio.

As we ascended the mountain, the view of the harbor quickly became one of the most incredible sights I had ever seen. Fishing and diving boats dotted the water, and the *Temptress* floated among them, giant and modern, like their hip, young mama. *There's my temporary home!* I pulled out my camera and started snapping pictures.

"This is nothing," the driver said. "Wait till we reach the top." He was right. No point in taking pictures through dirty glass when I could just wait a few more minutes for the good stuff.

When we finally got there after about twenty minutes, he parked alongside dozens of other taxis. "The view, miss," he said, opening my door.

"Thanks." I got out and walked to the edge of a barricaded cliff where lots of people, some of whom I recognized from my ship, were standing admiring the panorama. I did everything I could not to let my eyes tear up. It was so . . . wow. Impressive.

I stared at the curve of the bay, the mountains, the tiny little houses built on the slope. Paradise. That's what this was. I couldn't believe that I had no one to share it with. And yet, I enjoyed the fact that there was no one here to distract me. It was like the view was for me and me only. Okay, me and all these people. But it was easy to block them out. I just narrowed my eyes and focused on the scenery.

I stood there for a while, pretending I was an explorer who'd just landed here, wondering if this was where I should make my home, if maybe I should start a port city here. An uninhabited island all for me. I couldn't imagine what that was like, being so far from home in a new place. I'd always known my home. I'd always lived with my mom. Going to New York City was the most exciting thing I'd ever decided on, but I'd still have a focus there, a job to do. Get done with school, then come home quick. What about being somewhere without any plans or direction? The thought of it was exciting, but . . . scary. I could never do that.

"Shall I take a picture?" My driver's voice snapped me out of my daydream.

"Huh?" I turned to him.

He stood smiling at me, reaching out for my camera. "Unless you want to take a self-portrait," he said, laughing.

Yeah, right. Those pictures always came out ugly, everybody with big chins jutting out. "Sure." I handed him the camera. "Just press the button."

"Pictures, pictures," he sang, taking steps back.

I tossed my hair behind me, so the breeze could take it, and I could maybe have that windswept, tropical look in the shot. Maybe Lorenzo would think I looked incredibly sexy and put it up in his room, next to his games and DVDs. Somehow I didn't think that would happen, though. He had only one picture of me displayed, and it was from his computer club banquet two years ago. I looked young and dorky in it. So now I just smiled, because it was a beautiful day. And because I was on top of a lush mountain with a living postcard behind me. And because one day I'd show this picture to my kids and say, "See how young and pretty Mommy was?"

And they'd say, "You're still pretty, Mommy."

Cheeeeese. . . .

My driver, whose name I read off the license on the dashboard was Charles, drove me down to the shops and walking area of Charlotte Amalie. He explained there was a lot to see and pointed out each and every jewelry, antique, and art gallery he could think of. I don't think he realized I didn't have money to spend on stuff like that. I only wanted to get the feel of the town and soak it all in.

"Thank you," I said, and paid the cab fare, along with a few extra bucks for his tip.

He bowed his head. "You have a great day, miss."

"Thanks. You too." I watched him get in his car and drive off. I'd just spent about forty minutes with a total stranger, yet weirdly, I felt sad to see him go. Like he was already my best friend in this place. Funny how we can get used to new people just like that.

Main Street was the lively avenue of Charlotte Amalie. People strolled everywhere, like they had no particular place to go, music coming from somewhere and the aromas of different foods in the air. I didn't know where to start. I had so much time on my hands. I put away the brochures, resisting the urge to plan every moment of the day. I wanted just to enjoy it without knowing what I'd do next. I wanted to go wherever the wind took me. So *not* me. What was with me today?

I walked down a sidewalk, noticing how the town looked old and remodeled at the same time. The shops were nice, and the people really friendly. I didn't get the sense they smiled just for my business. They probably loved living in a beautiful Caribbean town where life was super laid-back. Who wouldn't?

I passed by a little shop with a sign on the glass door that read CRISTA'S PALMISTRY & TAROT. No! I had had enough fortune-telling for one week, thank you very much. Still, when I peeked inside, it looked like a warm kind of place with crystals, beads, little statuettes, and lots of books. I thought of the girls and what they might be doing right now. Maybe I could conduct a test of fate. If I ran into them, it'd mean we were destined to be friends forever, and if we didn't, then we weren't.

Honestly, I hadn't wanted to dwell on our future, but . . . I had no clue what was going to happen to us as friends. With all of us spread out everywhere, how were we going to stay close? Lorenzo would be flying up all the time, but the girls? My mom had told me about Judith, her best friend in high school. They'd stayed close in college, but after

Judith got married, Mom heard from her at first, but then little by little, their communication dwindled. I could not imagine that happening to us—except for Yoli, none of us even had brothers or sisters. We were all we had. But I couldn't see how we were all going to see one another more than a couple times a year either. It was scary just thinking about it.

So I tried to stop.

I wiped my eyes and went on, feeling more alive with the sun warming my face. I could almost feel my hair highlighting and my skin growing darker with the intense rays. I passed a coffee shop full of people, and ventured in. Coffee would be good right about now. Coffee, I knew and understood. Coffee did not change.

I got in line and stared up at the menu. Something cool or hot? Cool, definitely. It was a thousand degrees outside. I checked out the place, which was nothing like Starbucks. It was much homier, with framed maps and kid art on the walls, the kind of place where people could come in wearing ratty old flip-flops and not worry about the trend factor.

A tourist-looking man in front of me made a big deal about getting his coffee in a ceramic mug as opposed to a paper cup. I would've been annoyed, but the girl across the counter simply smiled and pushed a brimming saucer toward him.

Right then, there was a loud rumbling noise that sounded like an eighteen-wheeler careening through the streets. Except there couldn't have been an eighteen-wheeler on such a narrow street. I turned and saw the windowpanes of the coffeehouse vibrating. Under my feet, the floor rumbled. People had to hold on to their coffee cups to keep them from spilling. It seemed like a minor earthquake, except that would be crazy, on account of being in the Caribbean and all.

"What is that?" the man mumbled.

I watched the rings in his coffee ripple strongly, then subside. Yeah, what was that?

Some of the shop's employees rushed outside and started checking things out. Through the glass front door, I could see people standing on the sidewalk jabbering, some laughing, some shouting to one another across the street. The employees of the coffeehouse pointed at the brick walls of the building's exterior.

"Next?" a voice said. It was the girl from behind the counter, who looked to be about my age, dark skin, green eyes. She grinned at me. "Can I help you?"

"Medium frozen cappuccino, please," I said, then focused back on the commotion outside. "Did you catch that?"

"Catch what?" the cashier said.

"The shaking." I looked back at her.

"Yeah, it wasn't too bad."

I reached into my bag for some bills. What was she talking about? "What wasn't too bad?"

"The tremor."

"The what?" I looked up and blinked.

"Tremor?" she said, taking my cash and opening her register. "You know, an earthquake?"

My eyes popped open, and judging from the dryness

of my contact lenses I must have been staring at her pretty hard. (She must've thought I was on speed, which would've really been something, considering the wildest drug I'd ever done was Robitussin Cold & Cough.) I'm sorry, but did she say *earthquake*?

The girl closed the drawer and grabbed a plastic cup for my drink. "Don't worry, that was it. It's probably over."

Probably?

I could feel wrinkles in my forehead from my concentrating hard on not screaming my head off. Was there going to be another tremor any minute now? Didn't these things happen in succession? If they did, I wanted to find the girls and say my farewells.

I finally managed to speak. "I didn't know there were earthquakes here." Should the cruise ship be bringing people to places with earthquakes? Wasn't that unethical?

She nodded. "Tremors sometimes, but that's it. See those people?" She pointed outside. The next person in line and I both looked back.

"Yeah?"

"They're comparing cracks from the last one. This one must have made some new fissures out there."

I couldn't believe what she was saying. I had only been kidding when I said it felt like the floor was rumbling! A hurricane around these parts, okay, but an earthquake? Weren't earthquakes supposed to happen in, like, California? And correct me if I'm wrong, but last time I checked, earthquakes caused tsunamis, didn't they? And wasn't I currently standing on an island, a body of land notorious for being surrounded by water on all sides?

Hello? This wasn't funny!

A knot had formed in the pit of my stomach. *Crap. The girls arguing was nothing compared to this. Today I become part of a global news event.* I wanted to go home to Miami, to my bed, under the covers, where I'd be safe, but there was nothing I could do, no matter how much I wanted to. I was stuck here.

"Hey . . ." The girl scooted down the counter to where I was freaking, and leaned forward. There was something soothing about her smile. Obviously, this was nothing to her. "I'm sorry I scared you. Don't worry about it. They happen here all the time."

"All the time," another employee agreed over his shoulder.

"Okay," I said, trying to be okay. I looked around and saw a few other nervous faces. I reminded myself that I live in a place that sees at least three major hurricanes a year, so I should feel right at home. Besides, there was no safe place to be in this world. If it wasn't a tsunami or an earthquake, it was a hurricane, tornado, Chupacabra, or something.

I sat and sipped my drink, breathing deeply, watching the employees wander back into the store, laughing from all the excitement. *Whew!*

After that in town, everyone acted like nothing had happened. Occasionally, someone inside a store mentioned the tremor, comparing it to the last one that had happened a few months before, but otherwise, the morning went on. I did a lot of walking, thinking about tremors, imagining what it must be like to live in a place like this. It was real primal beauty: the palm trees, the banana trees, the wild-flowers growing on the side of the road, the kids playing in the street. The tremors. All a part of island life.

Were Yoli, Alma, and Kill okay? I wondered what they were doing without me. What about Raul? What was he doing on this fine, seismic-activity-filled day?

I followed some signs to Blackbeard's Castle. It was still exhilarating to do something on my own. Touring a city by myself. I couldn't get over it. I smiled. This is what Raul had been talking about. This is what he'd be doing next year.

I turned a corner and saw it: this simple round old stone building, like the sand castles I used to make with my mom when I was little. This was definitely a Kodak spot, so I asked an old couple if they could take a picture of me in front of the famous pirate's lookout.

I posed, big smile. . . . *Arrr, shiver me timbers*. . . .

The castle was next to an inn with a nice view of the harbor. Well, duh, that view is exactly why the castle had been built: so people could keep an eye out for intruders. It felt strange to be standing on the site of all that raping and pillaging that had gone on.

In sharp contrast, I looked through the iron gate into the garden and saw a wedding couple taking their formal pictures. The girl looked a bit like me: long brown hair, heart-shaped face, tall. Beau-tee-ful strapless white dress.

And the guy . . . the guy looked . . .

Familiar.

My heart stopped. I stood there, frozen. It was Raul. Wasn't it? Yes, that man's face was unmistakably gorgeous.

But I hadn't seen him with a girlfriend, fiancée, or anything. What was he doing?

I watched. And watched. He and his bride, from the look of it, switched poses, and a photographer with a big lens moved them around and took more shots. His wife—I couldn't believe that was his wife—was clutching his arm in this really annoying, possessive way.

Why was my heart beating so fast? Why did I care? It wasn't like anything had happened between us. I just thought maybe we'd had a moment, you know? And I mean, he seemed so interested in me. Not that it mattered, because I was a taken woman. Betrothed, like Yoli said. Just like him, apparently.

Off to one side of the pool, his cousins waited and watched them too. Or were they buddies? So this cruise was part of a wedding trip, or a bachelor party, or something. Yes, it had to be a bachelor party, otherwise he wouldn't have acted so free, so available, so freakin' single!

Damn it!

Why did my heart feel so broken? And where was my loyalty to Lorenzo, for God's sake? What was wrong with me?

For a second, I thought I saw Raul look at me. His eyes turned my way and sort of lingered. I hugged the wall and squatted onto the sidewalk. He seemed so distant, so different from last night. That's what I got for letting myself fantasize about people I barely knew.

Wait a minute. Was I supposed to be his last night of fun? Hit it and quit it? Me? Is that why he was being so nice? He was lying to me just to take advantage? *Augh!* My lungs felt like they were going to implode.

All that talk about doing stuff while he still had the chance. This is what he was talking about. Well, I was definitely one thing that would never happen to him now. Nope. Taken. Married. Off the market. I didn't know why—because I wasn't so far away from getting married myself—but standing there, watching Raul's wife clinging to his arm . . . I felt sorry for him.

Slowly, I inched my way up to the gate until I could just barely see them. Call me crazy, but he didn't look too happy. I mean, he was smiling and everything, but the way he'd smiled at me last night wasn't like this. This was more of a faraway smile, like maybe he didn't want to be there or something. I didn't know. Not only that, but it wasn't any of my business anymore.

Wait, was it ever?

DAY 5, 1:30 P.M.
ST. THOMAS, USVI—

I rushed away from the castle as quickly as I could. I would've liked to have seen it more closely, but there was no way I was going on those grounds now. Not with Mr. and Mrs. Raul there.

Why had I assumed he was single? Even engaged people are allowed to make conversation with strangers, aren't they? God, I felt stupid. And let down. Yes, I was excruciatingly aware of that. Somewhere in the back of my head, I had been hoping I'd get to kiss him before the cruise was over.

And I wouldn't have told Lorenzo about it. It would've been my little secret. Maybe everyone needed one of those, something to carry to the grave. But it wasn't going to happen now.

My taxi driver had told me about Coral World, which was supposed to be near here. Maybe I could head over to clear the fogginess from my brain. He said I might need another cab because of how hot it was, but looking at my map, I figured I'd just walk.

I ended up on a road that pointed toward the marine park. I'd seen pictures of Coral World's dome-shaped underwater observatory in the brochures, and it looked really cool. Maybe I could go snorkeling there. And never come up for air.

Just stay down there with the fish and stingrays.

And the sharks.

Anywhere without arguing girls, jealous boyfriends, and scheming cute guys.

Just me and some turtles.

In what seemed like an entire phase of the moon later, totally out of breath, and drenched in sweat, I got to the park's entrance. Oh, well. Exercise is a health benefit. The entrance fee was a little pricey, but I'd still have enough for a taxi back to port, and this place sounded like it was worth the money.

It wasn't Sea World, but it was nice. There were lots of exhibits where visitors could touch different ocean animals, like dolphins and stingrays. I kept away from those, just in case one was having a bad day or something. I made my way over to the Undersea Observatory, down a walkway that extended about a hundred feet away from shore. It was really the coolest thing there.

There were a ton of people there—families, teens, kids, old people—all having a good time, enjoying the gorgeous day. I couldn't believe I was here alone because my friends were dorks. I couldn't believe I had experienced an earthquake in the middle of the Caribbean. I couldn't believe my fantasy love interest on the ship was now hitched. I needed a vacation from this vacation.

Despite all the crappiness of the day, I wanted to keep exploring Charlotte Amalie. It was exactly what you'd think of when you thought of a Caribbean town. Everywhere I turned, there were brightly colored shirts and skirts for sale, beaded necklaces, sea-life toys for the kids. Kind of like Miami, but more friendly. That was the problem with Miami sometimes. Beautiful, but distant. Like a glittery movie star. St. Thomas was the girl who didn't realize she was beautiful. The girl next door.

An employee regulating the line for the Undersea Observatory said to the family in front of me, "You'll be in in a second." He gave me a little smile then looked back inside the observatory. He wasn't the greatest-looking guy in the world—he was definitely not Raul or Tyler—but he was cute enough. A bit taller than me, reddish brown hair, nice smile. Yoli, in her previous mind-set, might have liked him. I wanted to point him out to her, but alas, she wasn't here. She was probably at Immature World.

What was going on with her? Could one have an identity crisis at eighteen? She'd better get over it soon. I was surprised that Killian had conceded and left Tyler for Yoli's enjoyment. It wasn't like Killian to do that, but maybe she was finally starting to think of someone besides herself.

Observatory Boy let everybody in. "Hi," he said as I walked by.

"Hi." Was he flirting or being friendly? See? I sucked at knowing the difference. I vowed never to talk to a guy again just so I wouldn't have to decide.

I followed the group downstairs to the underwater level. Wow! Wow, wow, wow. This place was incredible! I mean, really. On the other side of wall-to-wall glass was a living coral reef. Schools of multicolored fish and plants, sharks, sea horses, the Little Mermaid, and her crab, I swear.

I'd never said "fascinating" before about an aquarium, but that's what it was: fascinating. It was another world. It was Coral World. I could stay all day. Seriously.

"That's a trumpet fish." To my right was the guy who'd let us in, leaning on the glass. He watched a long, funny-looking fish swim around.

"Oh, really? Cool."

"Yes, and that's a parrot fish." He had a British accent. Reminded me of Prince Harry.

I looked out at the parrot fish. It had a stripe from its mouth toward its eye that made it seem like it was smiling.

Maybe Prince Harry was bored, and I was the only one his age here. I glanced around. Yep, not a college crowd. They were probably all at bars trying to pick up Killian, or fight with her.

"This is beautiful," I said, watching a little yellow fish peck at the coral. "You must love working here."

"I do." He breathed against the glass and sighed. It

frosted for a second, then evaporated. "After a while, you get accustomed, though."

I couldn't imagine ever getting "accustomed" to this and looking bored like him. I could easily enjoy this for years and years. "Do you work every day, or just certain days?" I asked. What kind of a weird question was that?

He shrugged. "Only for the summer. Internship." He stared at a manta ray or a stingray—I didn't know the difference—that swam close to the glass. It landed on the sand and started burrowing, getting sand all over itself.

"Where do you go to school?"

"UVI."

"Where?"

"University of the Virgin Islands."

"Oh."

"Center for Marine Science and Environmental Studies."

"That's a mouthful." I laughed.

He did too. "Yeah. And you?"

"Pastry arts program at the French Culinary Institute in SoHo."

He laughed. "That's even more of a mouthful! Sounds good enough to eat, too."

"Right?" I blushed. Talking about mouthfuls and eating made me feel more than a little weird. Should I keep talking to him, or politely thank him for the marine biology lesson and move on to another part of the observatory? Why couldn't anything be easy?

"My name's Parker if you need anything." He tapped the

glass and started to walk off.

"Thanks." He'd made that decision easy for me, hadn't he? "Wait. . . ." I turned to him. "Can anyone do an internship here, or do you have to go to UVI?"

"I don't know. But there are always jobs, especially during the summer. Why, you interested?"

"No, I was thinking for a friend." Killian might want to do this. I knew that Coral World wasn't the most edge-of-your-seat kind of place, but she could work here during the day and party the local clubs at night. These seemingly laid-back islands all had hedonistic fun after the sun went down.

Killian could even go to UVI if she finally decided to study. One time she had said she wanted to be a marine biologist. Sure, she was eleven at the time, but think about it: She could even perform one stunt a week at Coral World to draw in bigger crowds. Coral World's hottest attraction: Come and see our real-life mermaid wrestle sharks. . . .

I made a mental note to tell her all about it after I got back. I had nothing to lose. Anything would be better than starring in a college-girl documentary.

"Well, see you around. . . ." Parker paused. I guessed I wasn't paying much attention to him. What was he waiting for? I realized, brain that I am, that he was pausing for my name.

"Fiona."

"Fiona," he repeated. "Great name. Is it in your family?"

I didn't know what was cooler: the fact that I was

surrounded by an undersea world within an air-conditioned space, dry as can be, or that this guy wasn't making a *Shrek* joke.

"Yes," I said. "It is."

"I like it." He smiled back. "See you around."

"See you." I turned my gaze back out to sea. Even the parrot fish was smiling at me. Like he'd heard every thought that had run through my head.

Good thing the taxi driver took a quick route back to the *Temptress.* By the time we reached the port, nasty clouds had moved over the harbor. I shuffled onto the ship right as the first drops began to fall from the swirling sky.

It was about five, and I was tired, no, drained from a very long day. I was also curious to see what everyone had done without me, where they had been when the mini-earthquake had struck. The first person I found was Yoli taking a nap in our cabin. I didn't want to wake her, but she heard me come in and opened her eyes. "Hey, Fee."

"Hey." I closed the door.

"You okay?"

"Yeah, why?"

"I'm sorry you got mad."

"I wasn't mad." *Well, maybe a little.* "Just stressed out."

She sat up and rubbed her eyes. "I know, but it was my fault."

"No, it wasn't." I plopped down on the bed.

"So anything interesting happen?" It was a simple question, but it felt like prying.

"Not really." I thought today might possibly have been the weirdest day of my life, but for some reason, I didn't feel like telling her. What for? To hear that I shouldn't be thinking of other guys anyway with Lorenzo back home, or that the tremor was part of Madame Fortuna's prediction and we should all heed her warning? Those things were already on my mind. I didn't need Yoli echoing them.

"I didn't do anything with Tyler," she said. Her confession hung in the air like humidity. She waited for me to say something. "We just danced, that's it. And kissed for a while."

I didn't really know what to say, especially since she was fishing for a reaction. She always did that. I wanted her to start doing things in life because she wanted to, not because of what others would think of her and not because she'd feel validation from Tyler picking her over Killian either. If she wanted to sleep with the guy, I didn't care anymore. As long she didn't feel bad about it later.

"He invited me to his room," Yoli whispered. My stomach tightened. *Jerk, for taking advantage of stupid girls like Yoli.* But I didn't say anything. Yoli was going to have to make this decision on her own.

"It's up to you," I said, and closed my eyes.

When I woke up, there was practically a party going on in my room. Yoli was blowing her hair straight. Killian was talking on and on about some guys who had invited her skydiving but how she didn't want to go without us and neither Alma nor Yoli wanted to jump with her. Even Alma was yakking about how she'd never do anything so stupid just to get with a guy and how Killian should seriously consider therapy.

My *chicas* looked beautiful, dressed in pretty sundresses and shiny, dangly earrings. Tonight was the Banana Bash, where everyone was to wear something she bought in town. I hadn't bought anything, but I had the hook bracelet from Killian. And the infamous sundress. So stupid. Like a dress would change things between me and Lorenzo.

"Well, look who's up." Killian sat next to me in bed. "So where were you during the Great Earthquake of two thousand eight?"

"You guys felt it too?"

"Yeah, we felt it too!" Killian crossed her shiny, tanned legs. "We took a boat ride around the island and were getting off right when it happened. But I almost didn't even notice it. These guys pointed it out."

Alma curled under the ends of Yoli's hair with a big round brush. "'Cause you're so used to vibrations, Kill, it didn't even compare." She winked at me secretively.

"Gross," Yoli said above the whine of the blow-dryer.

Killian turned to me. "So what did you do all day?"

"Nothing."

"Bull," Killian blurted.

"Why?"

"Because you're dead. You slept four hours. You did *something.*"

"Fine. If you must know . . ." I waited until all their

eyes fell on me. Then I let them have it. "I went to Raul's wedding."

Their eyes popped opened like in those old cartoons. *"What?"*

That got their attention.

"The guy . . . the guy from the dining room?" Yoli stammered, hurt in her eyes. "You didn't tell me that."

Yeah, well, I didn't feel like it.

Killian folded her arms, looking all stern. "What do you mean, 'wedding'?"

"Wedding," I repeated. "Marriage? Nuptials?"

They blinked, still lost in the fog.

"I don't get it," Yoli asked. "Who're you talking about?"

"She caught him getting married," Alma clarified for the moronettes.

Killian gasped, covering her mouth. "Oh . . . my . . ." she muttered under her hand. Not an easy task to shock her, I assure you.

"Exactly," I said, looking at Yoli, whose mouth was wide enough to let in flies.

I reached back and stretched, pushing my hands against the headboard. "Yup. This must be his bachelor party cruise or something. He was probably meeting his bride-to-be here in St. Thomas, because I don't remember seeing her on the ship."

Yoli looked disappointed. "Sorry, Fee. I know you thought he was cute."

"Sorry? For what?" I sat up, determined to not care anymore. "I didn't write my name on him or anything."

"Can I see your ring?" Alma said.

"What ring?"

"Exactly."

They laughed knowingly. Oh, so now I was the butt of their jokes? Yes, so I'm not an engaged woman and I don't belong to anyone. I get it.

"Ha, ha," I said. I bet Yoli was enjoying someone else getting teased for once.

But she gave me a sympathetic look. How did she know I liked Raul when I kept suggesting *she* be the one with him? *I* didn't even know I liked him. Fine, I guess I liked him. But he was a jerk for making me think he was available. Maybe he should've worn a hook bracelet too, or at least a big TAKEN sign, so there would've been no misunderstanding.

Killian clapped once and stood. That was it, time to move on—standard Killian Life Philosophy. "Whatever. There'll be more hot guys tonight. The cruise ain't over yet, baby."

"I don't want a hot guy," I mumbled, thinking how stupid that sounded. I wanted Raul.

Alma rolled her eyes at Killian, who laughed.

They went on primping and blow-drying like I wasn't there. Like I was full of crap. Because they knew, and I knew, that it was always about guys. We could pretend this cruise was for us and no one else. We could pretend I really missed Lorenzo. But a big part of our lives had always revolved around who liked who, the excitement of someone new, and telling the others about it.

And besides, even Alma was putting on lip gloss, so maybe I should just go with the flow. Let whatever happened tonight happen. If I met a guy, great. If I didn't, then it served me right for even considering betraying Lorenzo. Although, I had told Yoli two weeks ago that I'd cheat on him. Why did I say that? Did I mean it? Or was I just pissed?

I didn't know. My brain was fried from the sun. All I could figure at the moment was that it was time to shower and change into that dress—the forbidden, life-altering dress. The one, according to Lorenzo, with the power to change me into a promiscuous heathen.

Whether or not Lorenzo had the ability to tell the future was still unclear. But one thing was for certain: It was time to find out.

DAY 5, 10:25 P.M.
ST. THOMAS, USVI—

"*H*it me."

The dealer faced up another card on Alma's nine of hearts. A two of spades. Alma had eleven, plus the card facing down. If it was a face card or a ten, she'd win this one, considering the dealer's cards didn't look good.

Alma waited while the dealer added a jack of clubs to the hand of an older man sitting next to her and a king of spades to Tyler's. The older guy lost. He leaned back and sipped from his glass. I loved seeing Alma there, contending alongside a man old enough to be her grandfather.

Both Alma and Tyler faced their palms toward the dealer. *Stand.* The dealer finally revealed what was under her own first card. An ace! Twenty-two. *Sucker!*

The dealer lifted Alma's hidden card—queen of hearts. "Yes!" Alma clenched her fist in a victorious pose and shook hands with Tyler, who also won his hand. "Good job, my friend."

"Thank you." Tyler bowed his head then scanned around. A legion of girls were watching him play.

Alma had been at it for twenty minutes now, ever since we'd walked in and found Tyler already at the blackjack table, beating all his friends. Seeing no women at the table, she made it a point to sit and give the guys some competition. We all stood behind her and watched her kick butt. Now the only ones left were Tyler and this guy nobody knew.

Alma was up a couple hundred bucks. Not bad for a girl who learned to play blackjack and poker from a library book in fifth grade. We used to sit around and play one another at Killian's house, with her parents' nice card-and-chip set when they weren't home. Joanna, the housekeeper, would warn us not to touch those things, that she would tell Kill's parents when they got home if we didn't stop, but after we'd finish playing, we were real careful about putting everything back the way it was and polishing off the glass case.

Another guy with a balding head kept looking at me. I made it a point not to look back at him so he wouldn't think I was checking him out. He wasn't the only one I noticed giving me looks tonight. There were others, some of them cute. But after what had happened with Raul, I'd learned that you couldn't trust anyone on cruises.

I couldn't believe I'd considered kissing Raul yesterday. I would've become a home wrecker. Not to mention I might have wrecked my own relationship too.

A part of me wanted to get back to Miami so I could return to my normal life and forget all these immoral thoughts. But a part of me loved the lights and the dinging of the bells, the cocktail waitresses, the myriad of colors everywhere. It was exciting to be in a place where even the oldest people and I had something in common: We were all adults. I had stepped into a new chapter in my life, which was depressing at times. I could never go back to being one of those teens not allowed in the casino.

I looked at Yoli, who occasionally put her hands on Tyler's shoulders like she was his new girlfriend. This cruise had brought out that carefree side in her—the *what happens here, stays here* attitude. I wondered how their hookup would turn out by the end of the week.

Every so often, Killian would look over at them. I could tell she still liked Tyler, even though she had called him a jerk. And why not? They were both party people. But Killian was numbing herself with someone new—in this case, some nerdy guy she'd picked up during the boat tour around St. Thomas. His name was Wenzel, and he looked like a Wenzel, too—dorky hair, doofy big nose, socks and sandals, geeky enough for me to realize that this was another publicity stunt for Kill. She linked her arm through his, like they were a hot couple, and you could see the jealousy in every man's face in the casino: "What does that guy have that I don't?"

Let me tell you that, regardless of how confused I had been feeling lately about Lorenzo, I was happy to have a boyfriend at the moment. I didn't have to deal with this flirting-dating crap. I didn't have to fight Killian for Lorenzo's attention, and I certainly didn't have to wonder who my next kiss would come from.

Unless, of course, you liked that feeling.

Alma was in for another round. I scanned the casino, noticing how many people I recognized. Tyler and Edgar and their friends. Another girl I kept seeing who looked like a brunette Reese Witherspoon. Even Bruno and his girl-friend-wife-niece strolled through, taking a break from massaging and hostessing. It would be sad, at the end of the cruise, never to see them again. Like graduation all over again.

A familiar girl strolled behind the slot machines. At first, I wasn't sure if it was her. Then I saw her clearly when she came around. She was wearing a tight pink dress that showed off her investments. It was Psycho Chick, formerly known as Booby Girl. She was with one of her friends, heading toward the blackjack area. All the guys there stopped what they were doing and stared at her. Except Tyler, who was busy playing.

Did she still think Tyler was hers and no one else's? Or had she finally caught on to his multiple-girl bachelor status? Her brown eyes met mine as she got closer. I smiled a friendly smile. No need to cause a scene here. She didn't smile back, but she didn't look like she was out for blood either. In fact, she spotted Killian with her arms wrapped around Wenzel and seemed satisfied, as if she had taught Killian a lesson.

I wanted to lean into Yoli's ear and tell her to stop touching Tyler, just in case. This girl had told Killian to watch out unless she wanted to get hurt. How psychotic was that? I didn't want Yoli on her hit list. But before I could do anything, the girl ran her fingers through Tyler's hair as she walked by, and waved her fingers daintily when he looked back. She gave Yoli a hard look then headed toward the bar, where she pulled out a stool and parked herself.

So many girls vying for one guy's attention. And he wasn't even that great! I didn't understand it. At least Raul had seemed decent. Of course, he was a hypocrite now. Wasn't that worse? A guy who wasn't what he seemed to be? At least Tyler wasn't pretending to be anything but the party boy he was. Whatever. Raul was a jerk anyway.

After scoping the room for a while, Alma got up from the table and stretched. All around her, Tyler's buddies and Yoli and Killian congratulated her. I clapped with the others and put my arm around her.

"You showed 'em." I kissed her cheek.

"It was nothing," she said, like it was all in a day's work. "Now if only I could smoke one damn cigarette."

We headed outside to the covered breezeway, leaving the glaring lights and sounds of the casino behind. A curtain of rain fell with a vengeance. Behind it, I could barely see the lights of St. Thomas. All around, the wind blew, making a *whoo-hoo* sound in the breezeway. Back in the casino, I saw Killian and Yoli still behind, talking to their beaus.

"Any Smoke Patrol coming?" Alma asked.

I looked around for crew members. "Nope."

Alma muttered, reaching into her purse and pulling out a pack of cigarettes. "Just tell me if you see anyone." She pulled out a cigarette and lit it, sighing heavily.

"Couldn't wait till we're back on land tomorrow, huh?" We'd be in St. Thomas again for another exciting day.

"Nah." She drew in a long puff. The tip sizzled orange, then she let out the smoke.

"That girl was in there, the one you got into a fight with." I leaned back on the railing.

"Yeah, I saw."

"Yoli's being possessive with Tyler. She'd better be careful."

"Yeah, but"—Alma inhaled deeply—"that's Yoli's problem." She closed her eyes.

I leaned on a section of railing that was dry. "What are we doing tomorrow?"

"I don't know." Alma sounded like she'd had enough fun already.

"It's our last day before we head back," I said. We'd have two days of sea before reaching Miami, but still. No more ports of call. No more islands. "We have to do something fun."

"Yeah."

"While we still have the chance."

We were quiet for a while. I watched the waves crashing between the dock and the ship. It was a long way down. I imagined what it would be like to jump from up here, like if I were Killian or something.

"Is Lorenzo going to visit you up in New York?" Alma turned to me, eyes questioning.

"Of course. Why?"

She looked away and shrugged. "I don't know."

"That's it? Just 'I don't know'? What's wrong?" I asked the back of her head.

She side-glanced me, kicked her foot against the floor. "You promise not to get mad?"

"At what?" My hands got a little sweaty.

She touched my arm lightly. "Fiona, it's nothing. I only want to tell you something."

"Shoot."

She shifted her position and pulled a tobacco flake off her tongue. "You know I don't beat around the bush, so don't get mad, but . . . I think sometimes . . . Lorenzo doesn't care about you."

Okay. . . . Everyone's entitled to an opinion.

Alma focused on my eyes, gauging how things were going so far, I guess. "It's just that . . . you're always sucking up to him. I never see him do that to you."

"No, I'm not!" I said, smoothing out my controversial dress. "I even took this dress when he didn't want me to. And anyway, it's not about sucking up, Alma."

"I didn't say it was. What I'm saying is he should treat you better, not just like an accessory."

"An *accessory*?" I've never felt like an accessory. And anyway, how would a girl who's never had a serious boyfriend know anything about relationships? I couldn't believe she was standing there talking like some expert.

Alma breathed out a sigh through pursed lips. "Fiona,

before my mom died, she told me that in a relationship with a guy, he should treat you like a queen. The guy should adore you. And in return, you should give him the world."

I imagined a woman dressed in a gown with a sparkly crown, making her husband bow before her. That didn't seem like a very equal relationship to me.

I laughed. "That's nice, but it's not that simple. How many guys do you see acting that way?" She was so deluded.

"Exactly." She looked at me. "Because so many girls just accept whatever they get."

"Because what you're saying is unrealistic."

"Why?" She turned to me, narrowed her eyes. "Why is it so unrealistic? Is it unrealistic to make the one person who has devoted herself to you feel special, deserving of everything?"

I guess not, but still . . .

"How hard is that? Why do you think so many marriages fail, Fee? If the person you are with always makes you feel like you are the best thing on earth, if he makes you completely happy, if he was shouting his love for you at the top of his lungs . . . why would you ever leave him? Why would you ever look anywhere else?"

Was she waiting for me to answer?

"Why would you even think of being with anyone else? Ever?" she repeated.

"Because it's normal to look at other people, to fantasize?" Hey, I gave it a shot.

She gave a sarcastic laugh. "Fantasizing is one thing. But I saw your face when that Raul guy looked at you, and when you found out about him. I'm not saying he's"—she

bent her index fingers to look like quotation marks—
"'THE ONE,' but you must not be getting everything you
need from Lorenzo either or you wouldn't be interested in
other guys. And trust me, I don't mind that you are. You
should be."

"That's not true! I can check out other guys and still love
Lorenzo. God!"

"I don't know, Fee. I just . . . don't think you're in love
with him anymore."

"That's the biggest pile of crap, Alma." *What the hell
does she know?*

She sighed. "All I'm saying is . . . if Lorenzo treated you
with utmost respect, if he showed you just how much he
adores you, Fiona, you wouldn't think twice about it. But I
don't think he's the one for you. He doesn't love you the way
you deserve to be loved. So I don't think you should be putting all your eggs in one basket when you have your whole
life ahead of you. That's just my opinion."

"Fine," I said, trying to look like my eggs were just fine,
thank you very much.

But they weren't. And I didn't want Alma thinking I was
defensive or that she could never tell me anything either.
And I hated that stupid saying about eggs!

"I'm sorry," she said. "Now you're mad."

I uncrossed my arms and turned to face the mountainside. The rain had gotten harder. "I'm not, I swear."

Am I mad because she's so wrong?

The corners of her mouth turned up just a little. "You
sure?"

Or because she might be right?

171

"Yes, I'm sure." No, not really. I mean, Lorenzo's not perfect, but Jesus Christ, who is? If Alma thinks that's how a guy should always treat her, she'll be waiting a long time for the right one. Everyone's entitled to their own standards.

Alma blew out the last puff and ground out the cigarette on the ship's siding, tossing the butt overboard. She headed back toward the casino. "Are you coming with me?"

"In a minute," I said.

"Sorry if I pissed you off, Fee. I love you." She gave me an apologetic smile and disappeared through the glass doors.

I was so tense, I didn't know what to do. I couldn't believe Alma thought she was Dr. Phil now. When she herself had little to no experience, just a handful of theories she was holding on to because they were her mother's. Well, she was really setting herself up for some major disappointment, if you asked me, with all that queen adoration crap.

I slid my back down a column and planted my butt on the polished wood deck, stretching my legs out so no one could look up my dress. My legs looked nice and tanned. Looking in through the casino doors, I saw Santi and Monica approaching the exit. He stepped ahead of her and held the door open for her to walk through. She thanked him with a smile. He smiled back. They didn't even see me. Together, they walked out, holding hands down the breeze-way, their fingers linked.

Holding hands. After eight years and a baby. Even Lorenzo and I didn't hold hands anymore. *And* Santi had opened the door for her. You could tell by the way he did it, too, that he adored her. It wasn't just for show. And when she stopped walking to fix her sleeve, he stopped and tried to help her.

Like a queen. Regardless of what might be going on with them, he had treated her like a queen.

DAY 5, 11:45 P.M.
ST. THOMAS, USVI—

What was Lorenzo doing at this very moment? If he missed me, wouldn't he have called at least once during the trip? I knew I could've called him too, but he *had* abandoned me on the morning of departure. I thought he owed me at least an "I'm sorry." Land-to-sea calls *were* possible, just expensive. I'd read it on the paper next to the phone back in the cabin. Lorenzo could afford it. His dad wouldn't have cared, or even noticed, for that matter. God! How aggravating!

Maybe he was mad at me. But for what? For wanting to be with my friends? For wanting to look my age in a cute dress and not some boring, dumpy clothes? *Pfft.*

I took my time strolling toward the back of the ship. Under the deck's clear domed roof, the Banana Bash was well under way despite the rain. The reggae dance music was catchy, so I sat and people-watched for a while, wondering how long it would be before I saw Raul again, or if I'd ever see him again, now that he was probably on his honeymoon. Maybe he was still on the island. I shouldn't even think about him anymore.

Killian soon made it to the party. It was hard to ignore Her Royal Loudness when she walked in, as some new guy who was not Wenzel handed her a drink. Killian must be in heaven. Free drinks, dance floor, hot guys. Tyler was there now, sitting down at the bar with Edgar.

Behind Killian, Alma and Yoli came in together. Yoli saw me and waltzed right over. "Where'd you go? Why are you sitting here moping?"

"Not moping. Tired."

"You okay?"

"Great."

She looked at me sideways and smirked. "Okay." Then she got all excited. "Tyler's the sweetest thing. He's not an ass like you think. I know you think that."

I glanced at him over there smiling at a beautiful woman as she sashayed by. "Oh, yeah, he's great." I wasn't going to do it. I wasn't going to rain on Yoli's parade. If she thought Tyler was into her, so be it. This was her vacation, her illusion. I was no one to ruin it.

"He wants me to come by his room later. He and Edgar are going to have a cabin bash. Wanna come?"

"A cabin bash?" *You mean drinking, drugged revelry.* "No thanks," I said.

"Why not, Fee?"

"I just don't feel like it. Why don't we do something else, just the four of us? Why does it have to be with Tyler in Tyler's room?" Tyler! Tyler! Tyler! I wanted to blow my nose all over him already.

She shrugged. "I thought it'd be fun. Fee, we're going to be in college soon. We have to start acting like it."

"I didn't know being in college meant acting idiotic."

"What's so idiotic?" Yoli asked, not getting it. What had happened to the fearful Yoli I knew and loved? In a matter of days, she'd managed to disappear without a trace. Would she ever come back? Or was this it—was she on a new course for personality reinvention and I'd never see her again? I couldn't take this anymore. What was happening to my friends, my . . . *chicas*?

"Forget it. Look, maybe I'll pass by, if you're all going." At least until they started making whipped cream bikinis on one another. Then I'd go throw up.

What else was I going to do? Spend more time alone? Sit around with Yoli's brother? No, I had come on this cruise with my friends, so I should stick with my friends, even if they were selling out on me.

"So you're just going to sit here? Don't you wanna dance?"

"In a minute."

"Okay." She shrugged, and swayed off to the dance floor.

I didn't know what was bothering me. Maybe Alma had

rattled me with her theory. Or maybe things just weren't going as I had imagined. I'd thought the four of us would bond every night, toasting to our friendship, making memories every chance we got.

But here I was, a loser, watching them have fun without me. I was being a baby, I know. I should've shaken off whatever it was and gone out there, gotten a drink from one of Tyler's friends, and kicked it. I closed my eyes and took a deep breath, letting the music fill my head, the beat of it pounding my muscles like a sonic massage.

When I opened my eyes, Raul was sitting on a lounge chair next to me. Legs apart, hands clasped together between them. "Hi, Fiona." He smiled.

I did everything I could not to vomit on his shoes. I was so happy to see him and yet . . . confused as hell. What did he want? Why was he at this party? I couldn't say anything.

"Something wrong?" he asked. He was wearing khaki shorts, a Hawaiian shirt, and a lei around his neck. So hot. So damned hot, he could've popped right out of the pages of an Abercrombie & Fitch catalog. I hated him.

Um, yeah, something's wrong, you two-timer!

"Where are your *friends?*" I demanded. I meant wife, but whatever. God, I barely even knew him and I was sounding like his jealous mistress.

"My cousins? They're there." He pointed to the dance floor.

He had seen me. Back on the island. I know he had. At least I thought he had. Didn't he know why I was mad? "Is there something you want to say?" I asked. It sounded rude, but I mean, why was he talking to me? Didn't he have, like, a heart-shaped Jacuzzi he should be bubbling in right now?

Raul sat up straight. "I'm sorry. . . . Did I do something to upset you? I'll go." He stood to leave, disappointed.

"Wait," I blurted.

He raised his eyebrows.

"You didn't see me?"

"See you?" He tilted his head.

What was I doing? Was this really worth a confrontation when we hardly knew each other? But I thought we'd both felt something. I thought . . . "Whatever," I said. "See you around."

"Where should I have seen you?" he asked, not letting it go.

Okay, now I was confused. It was Raul I saw in that tuxedo, wasn't it? Getting married to that girl? "At the castle."

He paused, absorbed what I was saying, and looked up, as if the answers were written in the starry sky. Then he smiled. Slowly. And laughed.

"I'm glad this is funny," I said, getting up to leave. Ass.

He laughed so hard, he held his stomach. "Wait, Fiona. Hold on."

I wanted to get out of there, but I really was curious to hear his magnificent explanation.

"Remember I told you I was studying to be a systems analyst?"

"Yeah?"

"But that I freelanced on the side too?"

Yeah, so?

I folded my arms in response. I didn't know what his freelance analyst bullshit work had to do with anything. I glanced around, acting kind of bored, and saw Killian, Yoli, and Alma's eyes flitting over at us. They were dying . . . *dying . . .* for this scoop.

I put up a hand. "You don't have to explain anything to me, Raul. We hardly know each other. You were just being nice. I was the stupid one who thought you liked me."

"I do like you," he said in the most convincing way you could possibly imagine.

What a player! My God! "But you're married!" I shouted above the music. "Or did you think I wouldn't find out?"

He was stunned. But not stunned enough to keep from laughing. He laughed so hard, I could've punched him.

He paused long enough to catch his breath. "That was a photo shoot, Fiona." He tried really, really hard to stifle another burst of laughter. "A photo shoot." But there was no stifling, and he let out a jolly roar.

I still wanted to kill him. "Yes, I saw that, but . . ."

"I wasn't getting married. It was a photo shoot. Freelance work? That's what I do on the side. I just don't tell everyone that."

Wait . . .

"That wasn't your wife?" Killian was watching us again. Yoli tried sending me secret messages, but I purposely disarmed my ESP receptors and focused back on Raul. Those light brown eyes.

Raul laughed again, shaking his head.

"Who was it, then?"

"How should I know? Some girl I met ten minutes before we got started."

"So you're . . ."

Ooh. Now I got it. He looked so amazingly gorgeous in that white shirt during the sunset yesterday. And even now, he looked like a catalog boy.

"I model. On the side. But I don't go around telling girls that."

I felt a smile creeping up on me.

He wasn't married? You mean, this was one of those moments my future children and I would sit around the kitchen table laughing about? Fine, I could laugh at this. Ha-ha! Ha-ha-ha!

I was relieved, so relieved, but also . . . this meant he was available now, which made my stomach flip. Because now there was no denying I liked him. Wow, this changed things.

Raul reached out and took my hand. "I'm sorry you thought otherwise. But"—he laughed lightly—"that was funny."

"Thank you. Glad you thought so," I said, holding down a smile. I felt like Entertainer of the Year. "I'll be here all week." *So he's not married. What do I do?*

I replayed the afternoon in my head. Him standing by Blackbeard's Castle, the girl next to him, the photographer, his cousins waiting patiently nearby for him to finish, so they could go on sightseeing or whatever.

"I do a lot of tuxedo work. My agent pairs me up with models I don't know for wedding shots all the time. So he contacted someone in the Virgin Islands, since I was coming here anyway. The photographer thought the castle would make a nice background." We walked over to the bar, where he pulled out a stool for me. "You want anything?"

"Coke, please."

"A Coke for her, and a Long Island iced tea for me," he told the bartender and looked over at me again, shaking his head. "You thought I was getting married?"

"Well, it looked that way."

"I guess. And you were wondering why I was flirting with you just the day before."

"Uh-huh."

"You must have thought I was a real loser."

"Uh-huh."

He took a sip from his drink. "Well, I promise I'm not. Not completely honest about the modeling thing, but not a jerk. I just don't want people thinking I'm using it to my advantage."

I thought maybe his Adonis looks were already to his advantage, but I didn't say anything.

"So what about you? Do you do anything on the side that I don't know about?" He smiled, and judging from the sexiness of it, was having naughty thoughts.

This is where I was supposed to stop him from going any further by saying I have a boyfriend back home. "I have a boyfriend back home," I blurted. *Good girl, don't lie.* There, it was out. Now what?

"Oh." He peered into my eyes and blinked real slow. "But . . . ?"

"But what?"

"I don't know, you had a look in your eyes, like there was a 'but' coming."

I did?

"No, no buts. I just thought you should know." *Why, Fiona? Now nothing will ever happen between us.* But if I wanted something to happen between us, then why was I professing my loyalty to someone else? What was wrong with me?

Augh!

"Thanks," he said, pressing his lips together into a grin. "You know, you look incredibly gorgeous tonight."

"Thank you." I blushed.

"I can tell you that, right?"

"Of course," I said, watching his lips carefully. He had nice lips. Really nice, guyish lips. His face was half boyish, half rugged man. I liked him, and all I could think of was that he was talking to me and no one else. That, plus the fact that my *chicas'* faces were priceless.

For half an hour, we talked about what we'd done on the cruise so far. He was indeed here with his cousins, not his bachelor buddies, and had no girlfriend back home. He thought it would be nice to have one, but she'd have to live in Orlando, because he wasn't about to have a long-distance relationship. Which definitely scratched me off his list, because I was about to head to New York.

But that's okay. I wasn't thinking of being his girlfriend anyway. I just wanted to kiss him. One time. And have something to remember this cruise by. Would that be okay?

I looked over at my friends, who were dancing, still looking over at me every now and then to see what was going on. No doubt they were thinking I was being a bad girl, sitting here chatting away with a married man. I wanted so much to fool them, really give them something to gasp over.

"What?" Raul asked when I took the drink out of his hand and set it down.

I leaned in and noticed the slightly musky scent of his drink on his breath.

He lowered his eyes and gazed at my mouth. "Are you sure?" he whispered.

If I was going to do this, now was the time. It was a great party, and everyone else was having fun. Even Alma was dancing. Maybe she was right. Maybe Lorenzo didn't really care about me so much. And if he did, we could deal with that later. But right now, the *Temptress* was just that.

"Yes." I leaned in all the way until our lips were almost touching. "I'm sure."

Then it turned good. *Reeeal good.*

Hot. And deep. And well worth the trip.

DAY 5, 12:35 A.M.
ST. THOMAS, USVI—

"Ohmigod, ohmigod!" Yoli rushed over to me, almost breaking an ankle in her high heels. "Where'd he go?" Killian and Alma skidded to a stop right behind her.

"Bathroom," I said, sliding my finger along the rim of my Coke. *I'm a studette.* "He'll be right back, so scram, all of you."

"Oh, scram, now, is it?" Killian folded her arms. "'But this cruise is for *us* . . . we shouldn't be thinking about guys . . . this is our last chance . . . *blah, blah, blah.*' " She did a pretty good impression of me, except I never go "*blah, blah, blah.*"

"Fee, what gives? That guy's married!" Yoli cried, holding

up her palms to the heavens. "Is nothing sacred?"

I could have had so much fun with this, but I needed to hear their thoughts. "Well, you're not going to believe this, but . . . he's not. He was only working."

"Right, good one," Alma said, settling onto a stool.

"Seriously, he models tuxedos on the side."

"Is that what he told you?" Killian smiled all sneaky.

"For real. Do you see his wife here?"

"I don't know what she looks like." Yoli thought she was pretty funny.

"Well, anyway, it doesn't matter. It was just a kiss. That's all it's going to be."

Killian made her *tsk* sound. "You suck, Fiona."

"Look, I have to figure things out about Lorenzo first."

Alma pressed her lips into a sad smile. "Raul may not be around anymore when we get home," she murmured. She was right about that, but I couldn't just go and do something impulsive. Nine out of ten times, impulsive equaled stupid.

Killian put her arm around me and leaned her head onto mine. "*Pobrecita*, Fiona. She has her cake, but she can't eat it."

Because I am wise, I ignored her. Instead, I pulled Alma closer to me and leaned my head on her shoulder. "I never thought I'd do anything like this."

"I know. It's okay," Alma cooed.

Killian shrugged and did her fried egg sound. "What, kiss someone else? Please, that's nothing. Yoli here's the one breaking out."

"And why is being with Tyler breaking out?" Yoli raised

185

her eyebrows expectantly.

Killian snickered. "Look, Yoli, it's like this. . . ." The expression on her face said she was about to divulge the whole truth about Tyler, but I no longer wanted her to.

"No, Kill." I shot her a knowing look. I couldn't think of a compelling reason why Yoli shouldn't know about the guys she was hanging out with, except that maybe Killian was right and the information would only encourage her. But after what we'd been told before this trip started, maybe we should clarify what she was up against.

"No, *what*?" Yoli stared right at me. "You know, that's the second time you've done that. Is there something you guys want to tell me?"

Killian sighed, put a hand on Yoli's shoulder. "Nothing, except that Tyler and his friends aren't cutesy nice boys, Yoli. If you go to their party, they'll expect you to partake of the goodies, and I'm not talking cupcakes." She chuckled.

Alma ordered something to drink and laughed over her shoulder. "Cupcakes. Good one."

Behind Killian, I watched Psycho Chick round the dance floor. It looked like she was coming toward us.

Yoli, though, was digesting what Kill had said. Her whole face changed, like a great big giant answer had just landed in her lap. "You'll say anything to get me away from Tyler, won't you?"

Killian scoffed. "Are you kidding me? Jesus, Yoli, have you lost *all* your marbles? Or just some?"

Psycho Chick was almost upon us. I pinched Killian's side. "Bazongas, two o'clock."

Alma turned to look as Kill went on nagging Yoli. "'Cause if you have, we can put an ad in the paper to find them."

Alma accidentally-on-purpose took a step back, bumping into Psycho Chick and missing her foot by a hair. "Oops! What was that?"

Psycho Chick's mouth hung open as she shot invisible laser beams at Alma with her eyes. "I told you to watch out."

"Sorry, did you say something?" Alma glanced at her, all casual.

Psycho Chick decided to ignore Alma. She stared at Killian for a moment, then turned to Yoli. "Can I talk to you a second?"

"Me?" Yoli asked.

"Yes." Psycho Chick smiled. She looked different, calmer. She was actually pretty when she wasn't scowling. But I still didn't trust her. A few yards away, Tyler looked over at us, all curious. He smacked Edgar on the shoulder until they both were watching. "It'll only be a second. Over there?" Psycho Chick pointed to the doors that led into the breezeway.

Yoli shrugged. "Sure."

"No, Yoli!" I wanted to yell. That girl was pure evil. She had warned Killian to stay away from a guy who wasn't even hers. *And* she had spit on the floor! Clearly, she was a demon.

"What's wrong with right here?" Alma asked.

"I wasn't talking to you." Psycho Chick snarled her

favorite phrase. Alma's grip on her glass of Coke firmed up.

"You guys, it's fine," Yoli said, sidling away. The demon broke through us and followed her. Killian laughed, loud and annoying, so that Psycho would think it was about her. It worked, since she turned around and shot Killian another dirty look.

Strife and storms—they were everywhere.

Raul came back, pleased, it seemed, that his date had tripled. "Hey, the more, the merrier," he joked. I tried to see behind him, where Yoli had gone. What could the girl possibly be saying to her? I knew Yoli should've stayed away from Tyler. I knew it, and I didn't say anything. Now she was going to get her ass kicked for sure.

"We let her go," I said, getting off the stool. "We just let her go."

"Who?" Raul looked around.

"Nothing. I'll be right back," I said, and Killian started following me, but Alma didn't move.

"Leave her," she said. "She has to deal with things on her own. We're not always going to be there to watch over her."

"Yeah, but that girl is crazy," I said. "She could do Yoli some serious damage." It was true. And I did not want to witness the carnage.

Alma shrugged. "And what? We're going to save her?" She turned back to the dance floor.

"Uh . . . yes?" I blurted. Even though Yoli was being a great big baby on this trip, she still deserved a little action on our part. Alma's philosophy of throwing ourselves to the wolves just didn't apply here.

"Leave her, Fee. She's got to deal on her own," Alma insisted. Raul listened to all this curiously, not knowing what any of us were babbling about.

Whatever. I couldn't worry about Alma right now. Killian and I left, set to interrupt the meeting of the Tyler Girls. I fully expected to see Psycho having her discussion with Yoli, but there was no pink dress and no Yoli either. "Where'd they go?" I asked.

"No idea. Crap." Killian broke into a quick walk.

We checked each corridor, each doorway, running around the ship, weaving around people. Were we jumping the gun to assume something was wrong? Still, where could they have gone in four seconds? Did we pass them by mistake?

After we'd finally made one complete lap around the deck, we scanned the whole area and dance floor again but still didn't see them. Alma found us, now starting to look worried since we were not in possession of Yoli. "Any sign of her?"

Out of breath, I shook my head. Killian kicked a lamppost, eliciting looks from a couple of people. "All right, forget this. She's not here," she said, walking away from the party. She stopped to look back at Alma and me. "Coming?"

Raul was still lingering at the bar, giving me strange looks, but I didn't have time for him right now. I gave him a weak smile. He gave me a finger wave back. The three of us took off, Killian in the lead. We searched the casino, movie theater, dining rooms, lobby. Finally, we were so out of breath, we had to stop.

"I can't believe we let her go," I almost shouted, pacing across the busy, patterned carpet. "Are we stupid? We were supposed to watch each other's backs."

"Don't worry, she's fine," Alma said. I had my doubts about that. I couldn't see how Yoli could be fine when one second she had been with us and the next, she was missing with a psycho demon booby girl. Still, it was true we had to think rationally about this.

Killian leaned against a wall. "All right, let's think. She probably went off to talk to Crazy Head, then she came back to find us, but we were already gone. So . . . she might be looking for us just like we're looking for her."

Yes, that was it. We kept missing each other, going around in circles. Although it was hard to suppress darker thoughts, like that the girl had kicked Yoli's ass then thrown her into the dark waters of the port. Stupid, because anyone would've seen that happen. Didn't the ship's crew watch out for stuff like that all the time? Then again, I'd heard about a woman who disappeared from a cruise ship and nobody ever found her. And that college girl who went missing while on a port of call. Okay, this was quickly becoming a most unpleasant situation.

Why did we have to go into that stupid tent and listen to that freaky tarot witch? Were the cards actually making this happen? Or was I thinking the worst because I believed Madame F.? I hated that I didn't have any answers.

"Maybe we should've gone after her right away, like I

said, instead of waiting to hear Alma's brilliant opinion!" I fumed. "We would've found her before anything happened."

"Don't you dare blame this on me, Fiona," Alma barked. I couldn't remember the last time she'd talked to me that way.

"She'll blame it on whoever she feels like," Killian defended me. I appreciated her watching my back, but it wasn't necessary.

"All right, let's stop this!" I scolded. "Enough."

They both looked away. People were crossing the lobby in all different directions. Some glanced at us, but most were oblivious to the situation. We couldn't even ask for help because it wasn't that serious yet. So our friend had disappeared for an hour. So what? It happens all the time on cruise ships. Didn't it?

This was so ridiculous. I couldn't believe we had lost Yoli—let her go for one second, and just lost her. It was probably nothing. She'd probably talked to the girl for a couple minutes, like Killian said. Then she came back, and we were already gone. Except why wouldn't she come back through the same doors that we had gone through to find her? Would she have gone to the bathroom?

"We didn't check the bathrooms," I said, pressing the elevator button.

"No, we did not," Killian said. I had never seen her looking this serious. Was she having the same delusional thoughts that I was? Was Madame Fortuna's prediction messing with her head, the way it was with mine?

191

Considering the circumstances—that a few days ago, a complete stranger told us we'd be going on a voyage, that one of us wouldn't come home, plus the rain and the fights, and oh, yes, let's not forget the earthquakes—it was hard for me to believe that everything would be okay.

DAY 5 ½, 3:28 A.M.
ST. THOMAS, USVI—

*F*or another hour, we checked all the decks and the rooms we knew of. We even went to Tyler's room, where some guy answered the door and told us that the party had been moved but he didn't know where. Of course he didn't know where: He reeked of an interesting smoky odor, the kind that doesn't allow for much sensible brain activity.

We had pretty much exhausted all our options, save telling the crew that Yoli was missing. But that was the absolute last resort, which we weren't ready for. No, the theory that currently made the most sense was that Yoli was having her own little adventure and didn't want us to be a part of it. And since we didn't know the top-secret location of

Tyler's party, we'd just have to wait until she came up for air.

At which point I'd have to kick her ass myself.

The rain had stopped for the moment, but it was supposed to rain again tomorrow, our last day in St. Thomas. Killian jumped onto a lounge chair and stretched like she was trying to touch the cloudy night sky. It occurred to me that I would never jump onto a chair of any kind just to stretch, especially one that was all wet. I watched her long, thin body and wondered what would come of her in a few years, if she would still be nuts or if she would settle down and do something with her life.

Then I remembered about Coral World. "Hey, Kill."

She looked over at me with a worried smile. "Hmm?"

"I meant to tell you . . . there's this school on St. Thomas, it's called UVI. . . . "

"Uvi?" She pronounced the spelling and laughed.

"Yeah." I laughed too, but not really. "Well, supposedly they have a good marine biology department, and . . ." It had been today, right? God, it felt like days had gone by with this whole Yoli thing.

"Okay. . . ." Killian prompted for more.

"And I thought of you, since you don't know yet what you're going to be studying. You could study there for a year or so. And you could work at Coral World, the place I went to today." A burst of wind came through and picked up Killian's hair, swirling it behind her. She looked about as much like a marine biologist as Angelina Jolie might as a neurophysiologist.

"That's cool," she said, then yawned.

Okay, so I had hoped for a more enthusiastic response. Then again, it *was* three in the morning and I *was* talking about school. "They might have a drama department too. Either way, you could live in paradise." I tried to sound convincing.

Killian jumped down and did a little pirouette. "I already live in paradise."

I love Miami to death, but I meant something away from home. "You said you wanted to have fun before your life got too serious."

"When did I say that?"

"Yesterday?"

"Oh."

"And this could be a once-in-a-lifetime opportunity."

"Do they have a dance department?" she asked.

"Why? You're going to be a dancer now?" I almost laughed, but then I saw the seriousness in her face, like maybe I had just shot down her latest vision. "I don't know. You could ask. What else are you going to do?"

Alma snorted a little, and Killian giggled with her. I felt left out of some private joke between them. I always suspected that Killian and Alma kept secrets, ones they thought Yoli and I couldn't handle.

"What?" I asked, raising my eyebrows. "You're going to become an adult entertainer? Track Tyler down after this cruise is over?"

"I never said that," Killian shot back, looking slightly offended. Well, she's the one who'd mentioned the girly DVDs the other day, not me. We were quiet for a minute.

Killian went on doing pliés and arabesques. Alma gave me a sympathetic look.

"Anyway," I concluded, "I just thought it might be a unique thing to do, considering your options are open." If I couldn't come back in the fall to live in St. Thomas, at least one of us could.

Killian did a dramatic squat thing in front of me and gave me a peck on the cheek. "And I appreciate the idea."

So much for that. How dumb of me to think that Killian would want to spend any amount of time on a sleepy island feeding dolphins when she could be in a big city getting discovered. Or at least laid. I wouldn't mention it again. She would do whatever she wanted anyway.

It was late, so I headed back to the cabin, annoyed that I'd lost sight of Raul over this.

After a night of tossing and turning, I opened my eyes and saw Yoli's bed still made. My stomach sank as I quickly remembered our dilemma. I sprang out of bed and got dressed, even though it was only seven A.M. I would check Kill and Alma's cabin, search the ship a couple of times, and if nothing, wait at breakfast to see if Yoli showed up there.

If she didn't, I guess we'd have to take action—file a missing persons report or something. *How did this happen?* One second she was there, the next . . . gone. Her disappearance reminded me of those parents you see on talk shows telling their horrible stories of kids who vanished from the mall in the blink of an eye. But she could be anywhere on the ship or even in town. I tried to suppress a wave of panic.

Slipping on my sandals, I grabbed the card key. *Should I knock on Santiago's door?* I didn't want to worry them unless absolutely necessary, so I decided to wait until after going to breakfast. I knocked on Killian's door instead.

After a moment, Alma cracked it open and peeked out. "Anything?"

She shook her head.

"Well, I'm going to look again. See you at breakfast."

She nodded.

I took off, doing a quick check of my floor. Maybe I'd catch Yoli coming out of a room, shoes in hand, all morning after–like. Nothing.

On the next couple of levels, I found lots of bleary-eyed parents with young kids making their way to the early-bird breakfast. I went outside to one of the outer breezeways, and caught my breath at the view. St. Thomas was even more beautiful in the early-morning hours. Stillness hung over the island as the summer heat quickly burned away the light fog.

I looked down the hall and saw a girl in a pink dress asleep on a lounge chair. Psycho Boob Demon? I broke into a jog and stopped right in front of her. With my sandal, I kicked the bottom of her bare foot until she stirred. I imagined red vampire eyes shooting open, bloody fangs bared in warning. But she just opened rather normal, tired eyes at me.

"Where's Yoli?" I demanded.

"Who?" she rasped.

"My friend? The one you took aside to talk to last night?"

She seemed disoriented, then a look of recognition crossed her face.

I waited.

"I don't know," she said, and something inside me wanted to grab her implants and bop her over the head with them.

"What do you mean, 'I don't know'?" I said too loud for morning hours.

"I mean . . ." she said, her voice firming up, "I don't know. I asked her if she was seeing Tyler, or if he'd said anything about me, and she said no. Then we both ended up at his party, and the last time I saw her, she was leaving."

"Where? Where was this party?"

"Hispaniola deck, cabin three oh five, I think . . . I don't freakin' remember. Why?" Psycho asked, annoyed.

"Because she's missing."

I registered her genuine look of worry for a second before taking off in search of the Hispaniola deck.

Inside the lobby, the elevator couldn't have come any slower. I wasn't sure why I was going to the cabin where Tyler's party had taken place. Yoli was already long gone. Psycho said so. Still, maybe she had gone back and spent the night there. I only hoped her name wasn't already checked off of Tyler's *Do* list. What would her mom say if she knew? I couldn't believe she had gone to the party without us. We could've kept an eye on her.

I wanted this whole thing to be a misunderstanding and

have Yoli back to her normal, cautious self when we got home. We already had one nut to deal with. Yet somehow, Killian's nuttiness looked good on her. Double standard, I know.

The elevator doors closed. I pushed the button and waited, staring into the mirrored walls. Super dark circles loomed under my eyes. If I were Yoli's mom, I'd give her a good *fwap* on the buttocks, that's for sure.

The elevator doors popped open, and for a second, I imagined Yoli standing there, looking defeated and remorseful. We'd fall into each other's arms, and I'd kiss her cheek and yell at her at the same time, and make her tell me what had happened. But there was no one. I marched down a hallway and rounded some corners until I found room 305. I put my ear to the door to check for sounds of hedonistic activity. But all I heard was quiet.

I knocked lightly.

My heart pounded. What would I say to whoever opened?

Someone fumbled with the latch on the other side and propped open the door. A guy I recognized as one of Tyler's buddies. "Yeah?" he asked without even opening his eyes all the way.

"Have you seen my friend Yoli?" I tried getting a good look behind him, but all I could see were a couple of legs hanging off a couch. It looked like a suite.

"Who?" He opened the door more, leaning on the frame.

"Yoli. She has brown curly hair?" Then I remembered she had blown it out last night. "Straight, actually. She's been hanging around Tyler."

"The virgin chick?" he asked, opening one eye.

I was about to protest that comment, but what would that resolve? The point here was that he'd seen her. I just rolled my eyes. "She was wearing a sundress with purple flowers on it."

He thought about it, then started talking through a heavy yawn, as if I could understand him. When he saw my lost-for-words face, he repeated, "Yeah, I know who you're talking about. She left."

"Where'd she go?" I was getting really annoyed that no one knew much, but at least she was alive somewhere. But why wouldn't she have come back to the cabin?

"Pfft," he said, "who the hell knows?"

Hmm, okay. I stood there, hoping he might have more helpful words for me, but nope. "All right, thanks," I muttered.

"No problem." He closed the door with a bang.

Okay, that had got me nowhere. Some people had seen her, but no one knew where she was. Maybe she did go onshore. Maybe she met someone and went out to a club or something. Maybe she was having the time of her life at our expense. There was nothing more I could do. Except wait.

I thought of my mom and all the times she'd waited up for me when I stayed out late. And here was Yoli doing the same to us. To me. Well, she'd better get ready for a spanking, that's all I had to say.

DAY 6, 9:10 A.M.
ST. THOMAS, USVI—

*Y*ou didn't find her," Killian guessed correctly when I met them in the dining room. All the usual people were there, buzzing excitedly, filling their plates with bacon, eggs, pancakes, all stuff that would make me sick this morning. I glanced at Raul's table. It was empty.

I resented the fact that I could've spent a nice night with him, getting to know him better, but ended up searching for freakin' Yoli instead. "Nope," I said, plopping into a chair.

Alma sipped her coffee. Killian put her chin in her hands and glanced around. We didn't say much. The quiet was unsettling. What were they thinking? Did it have anything to do with a certain person whose name began with "Fart" and ended in "tuna"?

"Do you think . . ." I started.

"No," Alma said immediately. She gave me a hard stare over the edge of her coffee cup.

"How do you know what I was going to say?"

"I know what you were going to say, and the answer is no."

I was put off by her attitude, but I knew what she meant. Even if this was Madame Fortuna's little vision coming true, what good would it do to bring it up?

"We should consider it, you know," I said, disassembling my turtle-shaped napkin.

"We don't have to consider anything," Alma said. "She's fine. She'll show up."

Killian turned an empty glass over and wobbled it around. "You're letting this get to you, Fee."

"Of course I'm letting this get to me!" I fired back, and the people next to us looked over their shoulders. I lowered my voice. "Of course I'm letting this get to me. Yoli's missing! And someone told us this would happen!"

Alma broke off a piece of buttered roll. "Yeah, someone told us, but now you're turning it into a self-fulfilling prophecy."

Alma and her crap theories. "You're not serious," I said. "You really think we could have made this happen?"

"Well, if you go around thinking the worst about things, the worst has a way of happening."

My mouth opened to speak, but nothing came out. I saw the girls looking off into different directions. They seemed

older to me, like the girls I knew and yet . . . didn't anymore. . . .

Killian turned toward me. "If you come into something
believing it won't happen, it won't. And the other way
around, too," she said, wetting her fingertip with water and
making a chime sound on the edge of the glass. "Now you're
inventing all kinds of scenarios that fit the description."

"I'm not inventing anything." I was way too stressed to
be listening to this. "Anyway."

"Yeah, anyway," Killian said. I'd never seen her so serious or close to having an argument with me before. Why
was she telling me to ease up when she clearly felt the
same?

I wasn't about to sit there all broody with them. I got up
and headed to the buffet. Even though nothing appealed to
me, I grabbed a plate and piled stuff on, just to keep myself
busy. The next time I glanced over at Raul's table, I saw that
he was there, looking freshly showered and, might I add,
very edible. He saw me almost at the exact same second and
told his cousins something quick. Then he sort of jogged
over.

I tried to keep it cool.

"Hi there," he said, his voice full of hope.

I looked at him and grinned. "Hi."

"What are you going to do today?"

Oh, search for my missing girlfriend? "I don't know. You?"

"Probably go to Coral World."

"I went there yesterday," I said.

"I know." He smiled. "You told me. That's why I want
to go see it."

I bit my lip and tried not to look giddy.

"You disappeared last night. I was hoping to say good night." He walked alongside me as I turned the corner into the dessert section. Why dessert was a part of breakfast, I had no idea. But the color palette of chocolate, strawberries, and glazed cherries was making my brain cells feel fluffy.

"Sorry about that. My friend Yoli is missing, so we've been going crazy looking for her all over."

"Which one? The shorter one?" His hand measured the air. "With the curly hair?"

I looked right into his eyes. "Yeah, why? You've seen her?"

"No."

So much for that. I grabbed a couple of mini-marshmallows and topped off my plate.

"You've got quite a mountain of food there." Raul smiled down at my plate.

I kind of laughed too. I didn't know why I'd piled on so much when I had no intention of eating it.

"Hey," he said, touching my arm so I would focus on him. I did, and his light brown eyes staring at me underneath those sexy eyebrows were more than I could handle right then. "Don't worry about it. She'll show up."

I nodded.

I really wanted to take last night—the moment we kissed, talked, and had a good time—and bring it back for an encore, but today was different. Today, other things were bothering me. Like Yoli. And my life. And Alma's view of it. And how I had completely cheated on my boyfriend without any concern like some wicked adulteress. Not to mention my conversation with Killian last night. I really hated that a chance for something different and exciting was just sitting there for her, but she didn't want it. Hated, hated, hated that. She was wasting her life.

And to top it all off was this stupid prediction that may not even be accurate following us around, haunting our every move so that we can't even have fun without thinking about it.

Basically, if I had to take everything going on right now and make one of those horrid pie charts like they used to make us do in math, I'd say hanging out with Raul again would be nothing more than a sliver. Fine, more like a small slice. But only because he was so hot. Had this been one of those romantic cruises where the girls go by themselves in search of love or a one-time exciting fling, I would've said "screw it" and indulged in him, but I couldn't. I had to bring my friends back together. I had to figure out my lame-ass life and what I wanted to do about Lorenzo. Because this was really it. These were our last days.

"Thank you," I said to Raul.

He just looked at me. "For what?" he said.

I wanted to tell him that some of the things he'd said the other night had hit home. That maybe I should put things off and enjoy life for a while. That maybe he and Alma shared a brain. I wanted to tell him that his presence on this cruise was not inconsequential. But somehow I didn't think that's what he wanted to hear.

"For last night. It was real nice. But . . ."

Raul put his hands in his pockets. "Listen. You don't have to say anything." He smiled sadly. "I completely understand."

"You do?" I wanted to hug him, put my arms around him, and just feel him, but that might've been hard with me holding a plate full of fruit.

"Yes. If we see each other around these last two days, we'll play it by ear. I know you've got a lot on your plate right now."

We both looked down at my buffet plate and broke into laughs. My face muscles were both shocked and relieved at the change in direction.

"You know what I mean," he said between chuckles.

"Yes, I know." I smiled, as big and as sexy as I could. I really did like him, and I wanted him to know that. But maybe some other time. I could visit Gainesville or Orlando during a break or something. "Would you . . ."

"What?"

I didn't think I'd ever done this before. "Would you mind giving me your e-mail?"

He smiled, nodded. "And my phone. And my home address."

Whew! That was easy.

"But only if."

"Only if what?" I asked, making it a point to bat my eyelashes.

"You give me one more kiss before the cruise is over."

I smiled. I could handle that. "Deal."

He leaned close to me and kissed my cheek softly. I closed my eyes and felt the warmth of his lips on my skin. A ripple went through me. That was only a kiss on the cheek. Imagine the possibilities.

The girls and I finished breakfast then sat there. "So?" I asked. "Do you think we should tell a crew member now or what? She's not here."

Killian flipped a spoon over and over. Alma leaned back in her chair. "How about we tell Santi first?" Alma said.

In a way, I didn't want to. I mean, if someone told me my little sister was missing, I'd freak. But we had to. We had all day to look for her in St. Thomas. The ship left for home at six o'clock tonight.

"Fine," I said.

"Fine," Killian said too.

"Finally," Alma said, getting up.

I turned and gave Raul a last glance before leaving the dining room. He waved at me. I waved back. Man, it wasn't easy leaving that boy behind.

Out in the lobby, the ship's passengers were out and about. There was a sense of urgency, everyone running around, trying to fit ten more hours of island fun into their day before retreating back to their mainland lives. We stood there, waiting for the elevator doors to open so we could go tell Santi and Monica that we had accidentally misplaced their sister, when the bell dinged and out stepped a girl who looked familiar.

It was one of those weird moments when for one tiny second, you can't place someone, even though you've known her your whole life. Then it registered. My head wanted me to yell at the girl who'd caused us all a night of worry. But my heart . . . my heart wanted me to throw my arms around her and cover her in kisses.

And who was I to argue with my heart?

DAY 6, 10:30 A.M.
ST. THOMAS, USVI—

"No questions. Please." Yoli sniffed, pulling dark shades over her eyes. I got the sense she meant that for Killian, but I was the one who wanted to bombard her with questions now.

Alma leaned her head onto Yoli's. "But you had us worried."

"I know," she said, leaning back. "I'm sorry."

Alma put her arm around Yoli's shoulder and stared into the distance all pensivelike, as if these friends of hers had so much to learn. Yoli looked like she might start crying and laughing at the same time. I wondered what was up. I guessed she'd tell us when she was ready. Or at least me. I hoped.

She had changed clothes. She must've waited for me to leave the cabin so she could go in. She was now in shorts and a white tank. Where had she slept? What had happened?

I threw up my hands and let out an exasperated sigh. "Can we just have a good day, then?" I asked. My friends' faces fell on mine, a look of agreement and relief mixed together. "Please?"

Seriously. This had been enough. We were almost finished in the Caribbean, and we needed to blow off some steam already. Another massage would've been great if it weren't for the fact that we'd get separated again, plus I was almost out of cruise money. Then again, I had a Visa card, although I was only supposed to use it for emergencies. Was this a stress emergency?

"The rain's died down," Killian said, ushering us down the hall that led outside. "Let's go into town. Come on."

"Yeah, you can tell us about last night later, Yoli," I added for good measure, because she couldn't put us through a night of hell and expect not to dish out a full explanation at some point.

We walked through Charlotte Amalie, which I was already familiar with thanks to yesterday's exciting events. I made sure to point out all the things I'd seen and the cracks on the outside of the coffee shop where I'd been when the tremor had hit.

At one point Alma said, "And what is the precipitation here in St. Thomas, Tour Guide Fiona?" Killian and Yoli laughed, and I wanted to slap them. Fine, maybe I *was* talking too much, but they'd only circled the island yesterday. I was the one who'd gone into town.

I could sense that Killian was busting at the seams from curiosity. "Yoli, can you at least tell us what that stupid wench said to you?" she asked in the middle of a shell store. I was looking at a picture frame covered in tiny seashells. Before putting it down, I checked the black-and-white insert to see if the guy model holding a girl in a white dress up in the air was Raul. Nope.

Yoli dunked her hand in a bucket full of tiny smooth stones, lifting them then letting them cascade back. "Who, Giselle?"

Giselle? Psycho had a name?

Yoli shrugged. "Actually, she's not that bad. She just wanted to know what the deal was with Tyler. Was he with anyone or what. I told her I didn't know."

Duh, even I knew that.

"She could've asked me the same, instead of getting into a hissy fit." Killian leaned on a counter and touched a shell chime above her, making it tinkle.

"Well, let's see, you did flash your boobies right in front of her in an attempt to distract him," I offered by way of explanation, picking up another frame covered in glued-on sand.

Killian's tone got defensive. "She didn't know that. I might've not even known who he was."

Alma snorted. "Come on, Kill." She picked up two half shells and put them on her chest like a mermaid bikini.

"You were parading in front of him way before you did that. You don't realize how intimidated you make other girls feel."

Yoli did her hiccup-laugh when she saw Alma. I held back a chuckle. I really wanted Killian to listen and take Alma seriously, as seriously as one could take someone modeling a shell bikini. Killian looked at her and blinked real slow. "Mm-hm," she hummed, turning her eyes on Yoli. "So I've been told."

"But Yoli here is . . ." Alma paused for a word. She was going to make Yoli feel like crap for sure. "Nicer."

That's it?

Yoli took a stone in her hands and smiled to herself. Killian made a sniff sound, like she didn't know what to make of that.

Alma put down the shells. "Ten people can get ten different reactions from the same person, depending on chemistry, dynamics."

That was true. But my guess was that Psycho Chick— I mean, Giselle—didn't find Yoli very threatening, though I wasn't going to say that. It'd be interesting to see how Yoli would be in college, whether she would keep trying to assert herself like she did this week, and whether girls like Kill would go on pushing her aside. I couldn't slam her for trying.

We left the store when an employee started gravitating toward us. That whole I'm-going-to-bother-you-until-you-buy-something thing. It was already eleven A.M., and the sun was ripping us to shreds. Back home, I made fun of the little old ladies who walk around the city with umbrellas perched over their heads, as if it'd start raining right in the middle of a hot, sun-filled day, but now I would've paid good money for one of those suckers to block some of the sun.

We found a secret courtyard where four benches faced out in a circle. In the middle of the circle was a tree that provided huge shade and a plaque about a local townsperson who was responsible for keeping this area untouched by developers. All around were bushes of pink, white, and yellow flowers.

There was a collective sigh from us all when we sat down.

Quiet, except for the sounds from the street, and the quick bits of conversation from people passing the alley. I looked at the girls, each of their faces focused on something different, their minds all preoccupied with something their own. Yoli hugged her knees.

I reached across the bench to touch her shoulder. She looked at me with surprise, then gave me a sad smile. How much longer were we going to be like this, not really knowing if Yoli was okay, not talking about it? We could've been ripping things up and having a blast, but instead, we were sitting here like four old farts waiting for the bus.

I closed my eyes and almost dozed off, feeling the sun warm my legs and a soft breeze cool my shoulders. If I had been by myself, I would have lain down and taken a nap. Not enough sleep last night.

"I went to that party."

I opened my eyes and focused on Yoli, then away. I wanted her to keep talking. Killian and Alma did the same, looking off in opposite directions. *Don't interrupt her, just shut up and listen. . . .*

"You could have told me what they were up to," Yoli said. I saw she was talking to Killian.

"Yes, yes, bad Killian," Killian said, running her fingers over the white stitching of my bag.

"Kill didn't want to," Alma explained.

"Why?" Yoli asked.

"Because the way you've been acting—" Killian began.

Yoli cut her off, defensively. "I haven't been acting like anything."

"Yes, Yoli." Alma dug a hole in the gravel with the heel of her boot. "Yes, you have. You've been bold lately, and we didn't want you doing anything stupid."

"So you guys figured you'd shelter me from the outside world by not telling me the truth? I can make decisions, Killian." Yoli picked at her nails. That was the old Yoli right there. Defensive, insecure Yoli.

So did you? We were all dying to know.

"And?" I asked.

She bit at her cuticles and spit out the pieces. "And it was freakin' crazy. Lots of drinking, messing around. Substance abuse . . ." She sounded like Joey, our Bay High motivational speaker. "When I asked Tyler if you did any the night you hung out with them, Killian, he said you did."

"He what?" Killian shot up. "I most certainly did not!"

Yoli stared up at her. She paused to let things sink in with Kill. "I figured you wouldn't. Like I don't know you inside out."

Killian sighed loudly. "I might have had too many beers,

but that was it. They were smoking and passing shit around but not me," Killian said.

Yoli went on. "I wasn't even there like five minutes and this guy next to me started drooling from how much he had to puke. But then Tyler and I sat on his bed, and we started kissing, which was great, but then, he turned around . . ."

We waited. Yoli looked like she was trying to hold back some big tears. "And he grabbed this girl Denise who was there. . . ."

Killian clapped once. "That was the girl who was naked with the whipped cream!"

"What whipped cream?" Yoli asked.

"Nothing. The night I was with them," Killian clarified.

"Right. . . ." Yoli said. "Well, this time, she was practically naked the whole time she was there, along with her two friends. So then he turns to her and she gets on his lap, and they start kissing and going at it right there." She drops her head and covers her eyes.

"Oh, Yoli," I said. That sounded so weird coming from Yoli. I couldn't believe I wasn't there to help her out.

Yoli flipped up a palm. "I didn't know what to do. I thought he was so into me, but then, just like that, he was with another girl. Like I wasn't even there. And the worst part was that I couldn't stop staring at them!"

While Yoli dropped her head into her hands, Alma, Killian, and I gave one another looks. It was kind of sad that Yoli couldn't see it all coming. Oh, well, learning from your mistakes and all that . . .

"It was like I couldn't move! All I could do was sit there

feeling totally sorry for myself while Tyler groped this girl right in front of me, when I was the one he was supposed to be with. I'd thought he thought I was pretty special."

"You are pretty special." I put my around her. "It's okay, *chica*. The guy's an idiot, what do you want? You just couldn't see it . . . whatever."

"And besides, he was wasted," Killian said, squatting and looking into Yoli's face. She held her hands. "He didn't even realize what a wonderful gem of a girl he had right next to him."

Yoli shrugged. "You're just saying that."

"No, I'm not. Now stop moping." Killian reached up and tried stretching Yoli's mouth into a smile. This is when I loved Killian the most. When she was more than a lunatic, when she had enough sense to help us lick our wounds.

So Yoli had learned the hard way. One day, she'd look back on this and—

"Anyway, I had to do something. . . ." Yoli took a deep breath and let it out.

Huh?

"Uh-oh," Alma said, looking at me then back at Yoli. "Like what?"

Yoli sighed. "Like I got up and started dancing with the first guy I saw—this guy Fernie, who was kind of cute, though not as hot as Tyler, and he'd been looking at me during the whole party. . . ."

"Uh-huh . . ." we all said, waiting.

She smiled a sly grin. "And we really got into it. At first, I kept checking to see if Tyler was watching. . . ."

"Good. . . ." Killian urged her on. Obviously this was a

standard move from Love Interest Distraction 101.

"But after a while, I was having such a good time—this guy was so nice, so cute, and had a pretty good body, and was good at dancing . . ."

"Uh-huh . . ." I couldn't believe what I was hearing. Yoli taking the initiative?

"That I didn't even notice Tyler anymore. Me and Fernie, we started kissing. . . ." *Yoli kissed two different guys in one night? Wow, even I've never done anything like that before.* "And so . . . I went to his cabin."

"What?" we blurted right on cue.

Her eyes flitted from us to her nails. She seemed embarrassed and excited at the same time, like we would finally see her in a different light. "I went to his cabin," Yoli repeated, her smile lighting up her whole face.

"You gotta be shittin' me," Killian said, pretending to almost fall off the bench. "And? What happened?"

She went to the guy's cabin? She didn't even know him! She could've gotten raped or killed!

Yoli eyed Killian, trying to gauge if she was asking respectfully or not. Like she wanted to share details, but not if Killian was going to be raunchy about it. "We just spent the night together. We didn't do *it*. . . ." Yoli said like a little kid. She looked at her fingers again. "But we did a lot. And it was really great, you guys," she said, checking out our faces, especially mine. "And we're going to see each other when we get back to Miami."

I stared at Yoli. *My* Yoli, my best friend from fourth grade, was starting to do things even I wouldn't do: spontaneous, senseless things. "Wow," I said, and smiled, because

I didn't want to spoil things for her. She looked so happy, almost giddy. "I'm happy for you." Happy that she hadn't gotten into trouble, that she'd hooked up with someone who wasn't Tyler.

"Yoli, I am thoroughly impressed." Killian leaned back on the bench. "You started dancing with him for all the wrong reasons, but . . ."

Alma fished for a cigarette inside her bag. "But she ended up with him for the right ones. Way to go, Yoli."

They were right, but why didn't I feel as enthused? I couldn't wipe away a nagging feeling. Here was Yoli, who went ahead and spent the night with a guy she liked because she could, because she was single, and here I was running around the ship looking for her when I could've been with Raul, even though I really couldn't have been with Raul because I was tied to Lorenzo, and it was *really* getting to me that I couldn't do what I wanted because I had a responsibility at home—a boyfriend I cared for, but wasn't even that into anymore. . . .

Was I jealous?

Killian sat close to Yoli, trying to contain her glee, like she had just found a new best friend in her. "You would've done it, right? You can tell me."

Yoli's smile started out slow then spread into a big goofy grin. "I wanted to, but I'll give it a couple more times with him and see how I feel."

"So the whole time we were looking for you, you were with that guy," I said. And I thought she had fallen overboard, gotten killed by Psycho Chick, or was lost wandering the island like a ghost.

"Fernie," she corrected. "Yeah, but after I left his room, I went to Santi's. I told him where I'd been."

"You did?" Another surprise for me. She had gone to her brother, which I guess made sense. I mean, he is her flesh and blood, but it bothered me that she hadn't come to me.

We all kind of leaned back and groaned.

She should've come to me. I'm her best friend.

Then again, in our cabin yesterday, I hadn't wanted to talk to her after finding out about Raul. And she'd been so sweet, wanting to know if I was okay. But I'd shrugged her off. Fine. Maybe we both needed to lay off each other's backs.

I caught Yoli stealing glances at me. I was trying to read her face, too. She gave me a wimpy smile. Whatever. I guess Yoli was allowed to do something stupid, considering she almost never did. It was a weird feeling, though. I could've imagined something like this from Killian, but Yoli? I could hardly get over it.

I wanted to go back to the ship and stand on the very edge of the bow and raise my arms and let the wind take me, like Killian had done. I wanted to understand why all my friends and the things they were doing were suddenly annoying to me. Then I remembered what Alma had said about Lorenzo, about how some relationships run their course, and I couldn't help but wonder if that was happening to us four.

I reached to touch Yoli's shoulder again, to let her know that I was on her side, even though I wouldn't have done what she did. Or would I have? She looked at my hand for a second, then lowered her head until it rested right on it. I almost felt like this whole cruise had been a learning experience, that everything would work out for us from now on, and nothing bad was going to happen. I felt like I had taken this prediction thing way too far. But I wasn't 100 percent sure.

Which made me think of something.

DAY 6, 1:14 P.M.
ST. THOMAS, USVI—

"All right, let's go," I said loudly, getting up abruptly. The girls shifted around. "Go where?" Killian asked, stretching her legs.

"Just follow me, would you?" I headed back to the street, checking over my shoulder to make sure the ducklings were keeping up.

They scurried to their feet, picking up their bags, hustling. We went down a sidewalk two blocks then made a right. I was pretty sure I was going the right way. If the place wasn't too expensive, we could try it out. But first, it was this way. *No, this way. . . .*

I heard Alma two paces behind. "Maybe she's taking us to a mental institution."

Killian laughed. "Is that it, Fee? Is that where you're taking us? To a soft, padded place?"

Yoli sidled up next to me and linked her arm through mine. "Sorry."

"For what?" I huffed. *Drakes Passage, next street.*

"For not coming to find you. I just felt . . . I don't know . . . like you wouldn't understand. But Santi's neutral territory."

"What wouldn't I understand about you hooking up with a guy, Yoli? Don't sweat it, it's fine." Seriously, it was. I couldn't blame the girl for wanting to share her near-sex experience with her brother. Okay, maybe I thought it was a little strange, but whatever. No foul.

"You sure?"

"Yeah."

"What are you looking for?"

I stopped suddenly, Alma and Killian bumping into us from behind. "Here." I panted, peering into the little store-front, the one with the crystals hanging in the window.

Yoli. "A new age store?"

Killian. "An adult store."

"Quiet, fools," I said, pointing to the letters etched into the glass of the door. "It's a fortune-teller."

Yoli unlinked her arm from mine. "No. Uh-uh. Not again. We don't need anyone telling us more spooky things."

"Spooky?" I laughed. Only Yoli would say *spooky* like she were still ten. "Why would it be spooky? Just because Madame Fortuna was? Come on, it's the only way to see if she was right anyway."

Alma threw her cigarette on the ground and crushed it

out under her sandal. "We'll see if this one says the same thing."

"Yes, a second opinion. Great idea, Fee!" Killian bounced up and down. "So, who's this one? Madame . . ." She read the sign on the door. "Crista?"

Alma shrugged.

"And what if she does?" Yoli said. "What if she says the same thing as the other lady?"

"Then we'll know, and we won't have to wonder anymore," I said, my eyes following a couple of guys who passed us and turned to look at Killian's ass. Killian picked up the vibe and smiled at them.

Yoli sank into a squat. "Then we're all going to be on edge again, and I don't want that. We're finally okay. Please, let's do something else."

"Fine," I said, reaching for the door handle. "I'm going in, and I won't tell you what she says. Then we'll go do something else."

At first, Yoli's expression froze. But then she shot up and helped me open the heavy wooden door. "Wait." The door chimes tinkled as we pushed it open.

As soon as we were inside the cool air-conditioned space, a strong, sweet smell from a candle burning or one of those incense thingies hit us smack in the face. The store was nice and neat but homey too. There was shelf after shelf of little aromatherapy bottles and crystals, books and videos. It was all dark wood, but there was enough light coming in through the storefront window to liven up the space.

A woman sat on a stool behind a counter with a clipboard and a pen. I had the urge to go back and check the door sign again, make sure that this was in fact a tarot card place, not just a new age store.

"I'll be with you in two seconds," the woman said without looking up. She had short blond hair and seemed a little on the skinny side. Her accent was American.

"No problem," I answered. We gave one another nervous looks.

It really was a nice shop. It must be great to own your own store, fill it with whatever you want, and have people come in and share your interest with you. Maybe one day I would open my own *pâtisserie* here in St. Thomas. People could come in, order something, have coffee, and it would be this great superfamous hangout.

"Well, then." The lady put down her clipboard and stood. She smiled. "How can I help you?"

"Um, are you Crista?" I asked.

She shook her head. "No, Crista was my mother. I'm Helen."

"Oh, hi," I said, turning so she could see my friends. "We're interested in a tarot reading."

"All four of you?"

"Yeah, like together. Do you do that?" I said.

She made an unsure face. "I usually do one-on-one readings."

I looked back at the girls. Maybe this wasn't a good idea. Besides, this looked like it was going to cost way more than five fair tickets. Then again, that would probably be a good thing: We might get a more accurate reading, a real reading.

"It's that . . ." I started. The woman's eyes were brown

and deep. Her eyelids were creased by wrinkles, although she couldn't have been more than forty-something. But she looked kind, and I wanted to explain what had happened to us. "There was this lady who did a reading on us, and . . . it was bizarre. She didn't even explain anything, she just predicted what would happen on our cruise."

Helen gave a knowing laugh. "She couldn't have been very knowledgeable. Tarot readings don't predict. You simply ask some questions and have them answered."

"But she knew we were leaving on a trip," Yoli said.

Helen nodded. "Well, maybe she did have some ability to predict, but tarot has nothing to do with prediction. Why don't I read the cards for one of you? If you're satisfied, the rest of you can sit with me as well."

Alma made a face like it was up to me. Killian pursed her lips at me: *You do it.*

Well, it was my idea, so I figured I should go first. "Can they come?" I asked Helen.

"Sure!" Helen organized some little books by the cash register. "Some people have strict rules about more than one person listening in, but as long as your spirits are clean, and you don't sit in with sarcasm or doubt, I don't mind. Just open up, so I can read your auras."

She opened a flapping side door to let us through. "Right back there," she said, showing us to a room. I was expecting something cold and freaky, like Madame Fortuna's tent, but this was a warm room with a small table, chair cushions, pillows on a bench, some little statues, a lamp, lots of books, and an incense stick burning on a high shelf.

I was starting to feel like I could trust Helen. She had an easygoing way about her. I realized I hadn't asked how much a reading would be, but whatever it was, I was sure we could all pitch in, and I'd pay the girls back.

Helen hummed to herself, moving things out of the way so we could all sit. "Just have a seat. What's your name, hon?"

"Fiona."

"Fiona? Beautiful name."

"Thank you."

"Your mother liked a Fiona, I bet." She smiled.

How did she know that? "Yes, she did: the mom from *The Thorn Birds.*"

She sat down next to me. "Great book. One of my favorites. Okay, Fiona, how old are you?"

"Eighteen."

"Birth date?"

"December eleventh."

"Okay." She reached over and grabbed a basket, pulling out a bundle tied in a red silk handkerchief. She undid the knot and pulled out a very old, very used, and frayed deck of tarot cards. I wondered if they had been her mother's. Helen then closed her eyes and took a few slow breaths.

Killian, Alma, and Yoli watched from the sofa. They looked like they were holding their breaths.

"Do you have a specific question?" Helen asked me. "About anything in your life?"

I thought about that. Maybe, would I stay with Lorenzo? Or would my friends and I be together forever? Or whether or not that Death card was actually going to come true.

But the things on my mind were all sort of hashed together, nothing specific.

Helen seemed to sense this, or maybe she could just tell by looking at my stumped expression. "If not, we could just see what the tarot reveals to you."

"Yes, can we do that?" I said. "I don't really know what to ask about." Besides, this way, I wouldn't give her any clues to my personal life, and she'd have to do all the work. Was I slick or what?

"Take a deep breath," she instructed, and I did, closing my eyes. *Whatever's in my head, whatever is bothering me, whatever is going to be known, let it be known. . . . Let this lady feel it and interpret it for me, please.*

She shuffled the cards several times then asked me to cut the stack into three piles. I did as she said, and then she put them back together into one deck. This was something Madame Fortuna hadn't done. I was beginning to think Madame Fortuna had been a crock of crap.

Helen started with one card in the middle: a queen of some sort, to represent me. Then she mumbled, "This is what's behind you . . . this is what's above you . . . this is ahead of you . . . this is beneath you." She laid out more cards on the side of the cross shape she had formed. I noticed some of the same cards again but the art on them was different from that on the other ones, so I wasn't sure which was which.

She looked at them all for a minute, then let out a deep breath. "This is the Fool," Helen said, pointing at one.

"I had that at the other reading," I explained.

She nodded, but otherwise ignored me. Maybe it'd be better if I just shut up. "You could stand to toss the rule book out the window every now and then and take a risk."

Take a risk. Okay.

"Especially since you have a Magician next to you." She pointed to a card with a man wearing a gown and pointy hat. "You've been unable to make decisions lately, or you will be, I'm not sure which."

I looked at Yoli, and her eyes grew wide. I wasn't sure what that meant, but I was listening.

"Four of Cups," she said. "You might be searching for a more stimulating way of life. Maybe you're bored and are ready to look for adventure."

Wow. Well, I hadn't realized that until this cruise, but that sort of tied in with the stuff Raul and I had talked about. Maybe she would tell me if I would fall in love with someone who would take me on trips around the world. Maybe even Raul. I was definitely listening now.

"Here you have the Lovers, reversed." I saw what she meant. The card was upside down. "Which right side up would mean you have a strong partner, a soul mate, but upside down . . . someone may be deceiving you. So keep your eyes open; don't be blind."

I looked down. This, this really hit home. And I knew, *knew* that Alma was looking at me, or at least reveling in her message to me the other night. This was good. And true. And I believed Helen now, every word she said.

"You also have the Eight of Wands: disputes and disagreements, which is normal of course, because no one lives a perfect life, right?" She smiled.

I smiled back, but I was too stunned to speak.

"Or it could also mean a canceled journey."

Huh?

Would I cancel my trip to New York City? I couldn't see myself messing up everything I had worked hard for, disappointing my mom.

"I wouldn't worry too much about that," Helen continued, "except you also have the Page of Wands."

"Which is?" I asked.

"Which could mean a change of address or a journey that is delayed, or even someone who's untrustworthy. I'm not exactly sure. Were you planning to go somewhere this summer?"

"Only school," I said, feeling a knot in my gut. "And here, this cruise." I laughed nervously.

She tilted her head slightly. "Well, you're already here, so this other trip might not happen right away. It does say it's ahead of you. Could be next year or even after that. Nine of Pentacles is a monetary gift. . . ."

Which was maybe Killian's bracelet to me? I touched my bracelet and felt the smoothness of the larimar stone.

"Queen of Swords: You have some wise friends among you." She turned her head and smiled at my girls. They let out held-in, nervous laughs and smiled. I smiled too. Yes, they were. *Especially you, Alma dear. . . .*

"And see this?" She pointed to a card: a woman with her arm around a faceless spirit.

"Yes?"

"It's the Death card."

My heart seemed to stop for a moment then start again,

beating even faster. It didn't look like the Death card in Madame Fortuna's deck. Did I really want to know? "Which means?"

"Which a lot of people think means physical death, but it doesn't. You have to look at the other cards around it, but it really means change. A great change is coming. It symbolizes the death of old ideas, and new ones will soon begin. Which is fantastic! You girls are young, you just graduated. . . ."

I let out a sigh. Oh, my sweet lordy, I wasn't going to die! And neither were my friends. *Thank you!*

"So that makes sense, then, along with these other cards," she said, leaning back and taking them all in once again, making sure she wasn't overlooking anything. "Basically, Fiona, your other fortune-teller may not have known what she was saying, or she might not have explained much. But the tarot never lies, so that Death card was definitely meant for you. Or all of you."

I didn't know why, but I totally understood what she meant. I looked at my friends, faces I had known forever and had seen change over the years. I loved every single one of them, no matter how weird they were. And fine, maybe I was weird too, because I could really believe anything if I tried hard enough. Like Madame Fortuna. Like thinking Lorenzo really loved me. Which killed me, because that meant Yoli was right about the gullible thing. We were a mixed bunch, and didn't always get along, but they were all I knew, and I didn't want to lose them.

The room seemed charged with something I couldn't describe, not in a million years. But I felt like truth was with us. Not because of the cards, but because maybe we'd known all along what Helen was telling us. The cards just made it clearer.

"Change," she had said. "Risk."

I was scared of those words, but at the same time, knew I had to believe in them. What would my life be if I stayed in the same place forever? But more importantly, what on earth was I supposed to do now?

DAY 6, 4:30 P.M.
DEPARTURE FOR MIAMI—

We were standing on the edge of a cliff. Emotionally for me, and physically for all of us. I was glad to be back, this time with my best friends. My one reading had been enough for all of us.

"Say cheese," the nice tourist mom said, and she snapped a picture of me, Yoli, Killian, and Alma standing on top of the mountain overlooking Megan's Bay. She handed back my camera.

"Thanks."

The *Temptress* waited patiently on the other side of the island, surrounded by turquoise water, as passengers all over the island finalized their purchases, sightseeing, and escapades. It was getting late, time to start making our way back. But I didn't want to go. St. Thomas was the best place I had ever visited. Beautiful and charming, dangerous, breathtaking, and everything else. I really looked forward to going away to school, but I wished it were here instead of SoHo. Not that SoHo wasn't nice, I'm sure I'd like it once I got there, but . . . I guess I was really going to miss this place.

While the girls ambled back toward the road, I took one last look at the view, taking it in, recording every detail, just in case my life got too hectic, in case I never made it back. I knew that Helen had been right again—that I had a hard time letting go, that I should learn to take risks.

Like Killian. I could learn a thing or two from her. So what if she didn't know every next move she was going to make? At least she was having fun finding out.

And Yoli, who had called me gullible, though I didn't believe her. Maybe there was something to be said about her attempt to change. She'd basically made a fool of herself with Tyler, but so what? At least she'd tried something different.

And Alma, who didn't take too many risks, but had an uncanny ability to see all and always understood everything, even when we were dumb and blind. I had always felt like the one who had it together, the one who felt responsible for them, but there they were, all a thousand times smarter and wiser than me.

"Are you going to stand there all day?" Alma asked me.

"We're going to miss the ship." Yoli checked her phone for the time.

"We have more than an hour," I said, but I knew they

were bored and wanted to get back to fun on the ship. So I let go of the railing and followed them back to the cab.

"Could we do one stupid thing?" I asked, shading my eyes from the sun, which had come out from behind a cloud.

They stared at me. Alma looked like she couldn't take one more step as a tourist and would kill me if I made her walk up another hill.

"Just come here," I said. I didn't care if there were still people around. It's not like they knew what we were doing or even cared. I held out my hand.

"Oh, geez, Fiona, you really are a romantic fool." Killian laughed. She put her hand on mine. Alma added hers, just to humor me, and Yoli's eyes locked with mine, right before she softly laid hers on top.

I felt emotion rising in my chest, but I swallowed it back and took a deep breath. For my friends, for this moment, just in case we did go separate ways and never made it back again. Which I would, of course, die trying to prevent.

"Yo . . . Kill . . . All . . . Fee . . ." I said slowly, looking into the eyes of each of them. Yoli's brown, Killian's bright hazel, Alma's dark brown. All of them beautiful. All of them a part of me. I didn't want our time to end.

"Forever friends we will be," they said, and that was it.

I lost it. I started crying like an idiot. Hands over my face, sobbing like a great big blubbering baby. Great. Graduation all over again. Geez, what was wrong with me? Why was I acting all hormonal?

"*Ay*, Fiona," Alma said, taking my hand. "Don't be retarded."

Yoli slapped her arm. "God, Alma, you're such a rock." Which made me laugh. She put her arms around me and hugged me hard, but I knew what Yoli meant. I leaned into Yoli's shoulder and smelled the sweet scent of her coconut tanning lotion.

"A rock?" Killian laughed, leaning forward to catch her breath. "Yes, Alma, don't be such a boulder."

I laughed even harder, trying to control the snot that had already formed from crying. Yoli pulled me back and wiped my tears with the back of her hand. "Let's just go. God, this last day has sucked so baaaaad!" she yelled toward the bay, her voice disappearing into nothingness, here on top of the tallest point on the island.

It stopped me for a minute. I didn't think I had ever heard Yoli scream like that. Then Killian grabbed Yoli's arm and joined her. "Aaahhhhh!"

Fine. What the hell. It'd be one of those moments for my mental scrapbook. "Aaahhhhh!" I yelled too. Now we just needed Alma to join in. Cool, brooding, collected Alma.

She rolled her eyes, her cigarette dangling from between her lips, like a drugged-out rock star. For a moment, I thought she would actually leave us high and dry, yelling at the top of our lungs, feeling like fools, while she remained in Cooldom. But she dropped her bag on the gravel, pulled out her cigarette, and screamed, "Aaahhhhh!"

I swear we were sending birds flying off to find safer territory, but I didn't care. It felt good—so good!—to scream.

"Aaahhhhh!"

We finished, sucking in deep breaths, laughing and laying our arms out wide. There. We'd let it out. I smiled big, because it didn't matter what each of us was going through, we'd be fine.

Which is what finally made me realize it was okay. It was okay to let go and do something that my heart wanted. I knew it might hurt Lorenzo, definitely my mom, and maybe confuse my friends, but I had to start living my life for me, not anybody else. For once.

I don't know why I waited until the cab dropped us off in front of the port to say it. Maybe I was hoping voices of reason would sneak into my head and make me change my mind, but I let it out, right there, as we were getting back on the ship. "I'm staying."

Killian didn't hear me, and Alma and Yoli just looked like at me like they'd misunderstood something. "What?" Yoli asked.

"I'm staying."

She made a face. "Yeah, right. Very funny. Let's go." She turned around and headed up, but Alma knew. Somehow Alma always knew.

Her eyes implored mine. "Fee?"

Yoli and Killian realized that Alma and I were still at the bottom of the ramp and stopped, letting other people pass them. They made their way back down the gangway. "What happened? You left something in the cab?" Killian said.

"No."

"She's staying," Alma said, looking away.

Killian stared at me. Was I the one pulling the trick now? Was this supposed to be my payback for all the pranks she'd pulled on me in the past? "What do you mean you're staying?"

"I mean, I'm not going with you guys."

"What? Why not?" Yoli said, her mouth suspended open.

"Because I like it here."

"So?" Yoli blurted. "I like it here too. That doesn't mean I don't have a life I have to get back to now."

I watched the taxis take off one by one, their work done for the day. "That's fine for you, Yoli, but I don't start school until August. I have all summer."

"So you're going to stay here until August?" she said mockingly, like it was a stupid idea.

"I don't know. Maybe. If I like it, maybe longer. I don't know!"

"Fiona, are you freakin' kidding me?" She came right up to me and looked deep into my eyes.

I let out a breath. "I'm not kidding. I'm not in any rush. My classes don't start till then, and if I wanted to start later, I could. But for now, I want to stay. I love it here."

"You came on a cruise," Killian said, hand on one hip, the other hand gesturing toward the massive ship. "You have to go back on the cruise."

"No, actually, I don't." I explained that I'd read through all the cabin material, everything from phone calls to staying in a port of call. All I had to do was let the cruise ship people know what I was doing, so they wouldn't think they'd lost a passenger. "Just like you can buy a round-trip plane ticket, but not go back."

"Fee!" Yoli whined like a baby. "You can't do this! We still have two days together."

"I'm not going back, Yoli. I'm not ready."

"Lorenzo's going to freak when he finds out. What about your mom?" She played with her nails nervously.

"That's fine. I'll call and explain."

"Where are you going to stay?" Alma asked.

"I'll figure it out. I have a credit card . . . a little money." To get me started until I got a summer job. It could work. This was the U.S. Virgin Islands. They had the same banks as home. I'd be fine. I felt my heart fluttering inside my chest.

Killian did a thing that sort of sounded like a laugh of disbelief and a sob. "I can't believe this."

Me neither.

"It's you," she said, probably getting her first real good look at me in years. "It was you this whole time. The one who's not coming home."

I hadn't really thought of that, but yeah. I guess Madame Fortuna had known something, even though she didn't explain it very well. I smiled big. "And I thought it was going to be you."

"Me?" Killian drew her head in.

Yoli turned to her and laughed. "Yes, for being a crazy-ass."

"Right?" Alma laughed hard. I loved seeing her laugh like that.

"Don't give me that, Alma. I thought Psycho was going to kill you for sure," Killian scoffed.

"No kidding," I said, noticing some of the ship's crew

watching us from the top of the gangway, wondering what we were up to. Other passengers were still getting on, but it was almost time to lock up.

"You guys, I have to get my stuff, so just help me out, please?" I said, leading the way up to the ship.

"Don't close up," Killian told the crew members. "This one's defecting."

We showed our IDs and boarding passes and hurried up the elevators and down the halls.

So many different feelings were coursing through me: fear, excitement, doubt. I couldn't get a grip on just one. I didn't know what would happen with Lorenzo; I didn't know how my mother would react either. I didn't even know if I'd return home by August, although for now, that was the plan. Would I ever see Raul again after this cruise? Or was he just a passerby in my life, never to be seen again?

I didn't have the answers to any of my questions, but that was totally fine. For the first time in my life, I didn't want any answers. I wanted to follow my impulses, my instincts, instead of a laid-out plan. Which gave me a huge rush of adrenaline. I felt very much alive.

And it was about time.

DAY 6, 5:15 P.M.
DEPARTURE FOR MIAMI—

Or not.

"She can always sleep on the beach her first night." Santi laughed, watching me pack. Everyone was there, watching me pack. I felt like an actress in her dressing room, surrounded by admirers.

"Oh, sure," Monica joked. "That sounds nice: St. Thomas on five dollars a day." She turned to me. "We'll give you enough for a couple of nights, sweetie. Or else your mother will never forgive us."

My mother. *Oh, man.* The reality of this was starting to sink in. She was definitely going to flip, if she didn't flat-out croak from the shock. "I have some money," I said, stuffing a pair of flip-flops into the side pocket of my carry-on.

Monica shook her head. "No, take it, or I won't feel right. You can pay us back later, when you're a famous chef with your own show, like that guy. . . ."

She could be talking about any number of guys, but I appreciated what she was telling me. It was nice to hear someone believe in me, that this would all turn out for the best.

"Me too, Fee. I'll give you enough cash to last a while." Killian's leg bounced nervously on the bed. She was so excited, I couldn't refuse. Was this the monetary gift Helen mentioned? "What are you going to do? Where will you work? What about that place you told me about?"

"Which place?" I looked up from my bags. "Coral World? Yeah, maybe." I thought about that. That would be really nice, actually. And I already knew someone there. Prince Harry. He could be my first friend. I could work there mornings and go to the beach in the afternoons. Or work at the coffee place, or anywhere, really. The possibilities were making my head spin.

Alma didn't say much. But she did sit there on the edge of Yoli's bed, grinning at me, something new in her face. Like maybe she admired me for once, instead of me admiring her. Like I was a new person to her. Hell, I was a new person to me.

But Yoli didn't look too happy. She seemed on the verge of tears. I knew she was disappointed. She thought she had a couple more weeks to spend with me before taking off for Tallahassee. But I had to do this. Once back home, I'd get sucked into a rut and never make a decision like this again.

It was basically now or never.

I wanted to give the girls something like Killian had given us, but I didn't want to spend too much now that I was going to make my first real move as an adult. But I had already thought of something, so I led them through the corridors to one of the photo shops and found the picture they'd taken of us when we first came on the *Temptress*.

It took twenty minutes to find the photo, so long that I thought the ship would leave with me on it, and I'd lose my chance to stay on St. Thomas, but eventually we found it. Four silly girls huddled together, smiling, happy, excited to be embarking on a new adventure. I would put it up in my new living quarters, wherever they may be, and look at it every day. It had been taken only six days ago, but I felt like a lifetime had passed. I was already a different person. I had three copies made and gave one to each of my *chicas*.

Santi carried my bag and cosigned some forms at the purser's office. I could tell he was nervous about letting me go, being our chaperone and all, but from the way he kept shaking his head and sighing all over the place, I could also tell he knew that I was an adult and could legally make my own decision. I swore to defend him when I had it out with my mom on the phone. He deserved that, at least. For helping me see that Lorenzo was not like him at all. Not one bit.

The ship would be leaving in ten minutes.

The purser had called a cab to take me to a nearby hotel for my first night, then I'd take it from there. I could either stay a couple more nights or I could move into a furnished apartment. He said there were many, since so many people owned places on the island but didn't live there full-time, renting out their places the rest of the year. Either way, I'd find something.

I'll be fine, I kept telling myself. No one ever died from not knowing what their next move would be. I might even find a *pâtisserie* and see if they'd hire me as side help. Anything was possible.

"Oh! Wait, wait, wait, wait. . . ," Killian said. She let go of my hair, which she'd been twisting, and rushed off into the lobby.

I hugged Santi and Monica first, thanking them for being so understanding and for being cool chaperones, and for the cash they gave me, which they really didn't have to do. Then I looked at Alma. She pressed her lips into a smile, and when I saw her eyes water up, I knew I was doing the right thing. She hugged me hard and kissed my cheek. "We'll see you soon, okay?" I never took her for being the positive one, but she made me feel like this wasn't an end. Just a break.

Whereas Yoli was already crying, and I had to hold her to keep her from shaking. Santi held her shoulders from behind, kneading them to make her relax. "I'm going to be fine," I said into her ear. "They have phones. I'll find an e-café. We'll be in touch, don't worry." But I felt like nothing I could tell her would make her stop shaking. I hugged her hard.

Killian came back, holding the hand of one superhot male. He didn't really fit the picture because he wasn't one of my best friends, but so what. I owed him a kiss, and a promise was a promise.

Raul pulled me aside. "She said you're staying?"

"Yep." I smiled.

He took my hand, pressed his forehead onto mine. "Wow. That's really gutsy of you."

"Well, it might only be for a few weeks, or maybe the whole summer, I'm not sure. That's the point. For once, I don't want to know. . . . I just want to have fun finding out."

"That's exactly right. You're . . ." He paused to find the right word, but some guys aren't always the best at finding the right word, especially when they're studying to be systems analysts, whatever that meant. "Awesome."

I smiled. I could deal with *awesome*. I leaned up and pressed my lips against his, feeling them one last time. For now anyway. His kisses were too good not to keep in touch. I would definitely have to get a phone and a computer soon. "Take care," I said.

"You too. We'll miss you the rest of the cruise. I'll give your friends all my home info."

"Okay."

He smiled and backed up, letting my hands fall to my sides. I watched him cross the lobby and disappear down a hall.

Sigh.

Okay, so maybe I should stay!

No!

Yes!

No!

I saw Monica and Santi giving each other weird looks. I'd forgotten that they didn't know about Raul. Oh, well. The girls would fill them in. I grabbed my skinny Killian and hugged her hard. We did a little spin and dance, laughing and laughing. "I can't believe you're crazier than me," she said.

"Stay with me, Kill," I said.

"I can't."

"Why not?"

"Not enough going on for me here, Fee."

I nodded. I knew that Kill needed a more action-packed place, but it was worth a shot.

"Watch for us on the deck, okay?" Killian said, pointing. "Right up there, on this side."

"I will."

She planted ten kisses on my cheek in succession like a mom leaving her five-year-old at the kindergarten door, then did a little wave. This was it. An officer smiled at me, showing me the way out. I was the only one leaving the ship. And once I was out, that would be it. No turning back. No regrets. And if I did have some, I could book a flight home and that'd be it. No big deal.

I'll be fine, I thought again, backing into the hallway. They all waved, and I turned around and walked into the tunnel. At the end of the gangway, I jumped out onto the concrete, right as a port worker helped push it up. He gave the all-clear signal to the crew above.

"A lot of people like it here," he said to me.

So I wasn't the only one to do this before, but I definitely felt like it.

I leaned against a low brick wall, where some locals and taxi drivers were sitting, feeding seagulls and watching the ship's departure procedures. I tried to push back some feelings of being removed, of being where I wasn't quite supposed to be. Watching the *Temptress* get ready to sail without me was making me jittery. But all I had to do was turn my head and see the island that would be my home for a while, and I got excited all over again.

Yes, I was doing the right thing. I knew it. And I wouldn't be sorry.

I found the taxi the purser had hailed for me. The driver seemed harmless enough, a young guy my age. "Could you wait one second?" I asked him.

"No problem," he said, taking my bags and putting them in the trunk.

I scanned the ship's deck frantically to get one last glimpse of my girls, Santi, and Monica. After a few minutes, they all appeared on the upper deck. Killian was pushing someone aside so they could see me better. I laughed. That girl would never change. Or maybe she would, who knew. They waved and whistled and jumped. Then the ship's horn blared, drowning them out, and I finally got my *Love Boat* moment.

When the *Temptress* slowly pulled away from the port, I felt a heaviness go through me. I'd be fine. I was doing this. I was really doing this. I watched them wave and cry, "Love you, Fiona! Love you!" I blew kisses at them, and suddenly remembered my camera. I fumbled around in my bag and found it, snapping five, six last pictures of them.

Sometimes you just recognize a moment you'll never forget. This was one of them. My eyes, ears, brain, everything soaked in the whole scene: the ship leaving with my friends on it, the mountains in the background, the darkening orange-and-purple sky behind them. I never expected my cruise to end this way, but I wasn't totally surprised by it either. I'd been ready for a change, even before the trip started. I guess I didn't need a fortune-teller to tell me that.

I gave one final wave to the girls and the *Temptress*. Her horn blasted again, the depth of its tone shaking my insides. I felt for my hook bracelet and faced it out. Then, taking a superdeep breath and letting it out fast, I opened the back door to the rumbling taxi and stepped inside.

ACKNOWLEDGMENTS

This book would not have been possible without the following people:

My agent, Steven Chudney, who is not only smart but talented and a good cook too. Thank you for guiding me over the last five years.

My editor, Sarah Sevier, for having the incredibly difficult job of making a book go from good to great. Your expertise is much appreciated.

Leann Heywood, for editing the first revision and remaining my good friend despite it.

My husband, Chris Nuñez, who reads everything I put in front of him even if it puts him to sleep first. I love you.

My mother, Yolanda, who has always been and continues to be my biggest supporter. There are no words.

Adrienne Sylver, Danielle Joseph, and the rest of the South Florida writers' group for your invaluable feedback.

All my friends and family for putting up with my not answering the phone.

And last, but not least, my dog, Chewy, who let me rest my feet on him as I wrote this book at the computer. This footstool is just not the same. Thank you, and enjoy.